THE DETECTIVE O'MALLEY MEGAPACK®

THE DETECTIVE O'MALLEY MEGAPACK®

WILLIAM MacHARG

WILDSIDE PRESS

COPYRIGHT INFO

Contents

THE GREEN PAINT

Originally published in *Collier's*, November 29, 1930.

"This one," O'Malley said, "is a case where a guy got stabbed and was found floating in the harbor. They couldn't tell who he was because he didn't have no clothes on. But now they got the clothes, so they put me on the case. I won't find out nothing, but I got to go look at the clothes."

"Where'd they find those?" I asked.

"They were in the harbor too. They'd had a weight on 'em but a steamer broke 'em loose."

The clothes were at the police station. We looked at them. They were of fine quality and make, but of old style and worn. The tailor's label had been cut out of them. There were small spots of green paint on them. The clothes had been tied into a bundle with a heavy cord and the police had cut the cord so as to preserve the knots. There was no doubt they were the dead man's clothes because they had a picture of him and the holes in the clothes corresponded with the stab wounds. He was a fine-looking man of middle age, and he had been stabbed several times.

"Those are neat knots," I commented. "Whoever tied them knew his ropes."

"You're good!"

We went back into the outer office.

"They identified that guy yet?" O'Malley asked the sergeant.

"They have now," the sergeant answered. "I just got it. There was a laundry mark on his shirt and they traced it down. They got who he was and where he lived, and the key in the clothes unlocked his door. Marlind, the name is."

He gave us the address.

"Well," O'Malley said, "I suppose we got to go out there."

We went. It was one of a row of brownstone fronts remodeled into cheap apartments. The basement floors were shops; at the street end was the river. Marlind had had a single room, with easy-chair and reading lamp and books. There were several pictures of two very beautiful women. Nothing had happened in the room, for it was all in perfect order, but there was a cop there waiting to see who came.

We went across the hall and rang a bell.

"You know Mr. Marlind?" O'Malley asked the woman.

"To say howdy-do to. That's all anybody knew him."

"When did you see him last?"

"Four days ago."

"Who used to come to see him?"

"I never knew of anybody coming to see him."

We rang all the bells and asked everybody the same questions and then we went out into the street and asked the storekeepers. Everybody knew Marlind to speak to but nobody knew anything about him; he never had any visitors.

"This guy," O'Malley said, "seems to have been what they call a recluse. That means a guy that a smash has been handed to, so that he's lost interest and stopped trying. He said good morning to everybody but nothing else, and when he wanted company he sat in a store and talked with the storekeeper; and he spent his evenings home. How you going to figure who'd kill a guy like that? You can't."

* * * *

The last place we came to was a Chinese laundry. The floor was freshly painted green. The Chinaman was ironing and I didn't like his looks.

"You're all painted up here," O'Malley said to him. "Who done that?"

"Me."

"When did you do it?"

"One time."

He wouldn't answer anything else. We went out and walked all around to find where the Chinaman bought his paint, but there was no paint store in the neighborhood. At the end of the street, on the river, was a place that sold marine stores and, in back of it, in a big clean room with a concrete floor two men were working on a boat—a big man and a smaller one; the small man had red hair. On a shelf on the wall were cans of paint.

"You sell the Chinaman some paint?" O'Malley inquired of them.

"Sure," the big man answered. "We were paintin' her hull and the Chinaman came in and wanted some paint of that color and I sold him some." The hull was painted green.

"When was that?"

"Four days ago."

"You know Marlind?"

"Sure," the big man said. "He comes and sits here. Anything happened to him?"

"That makes the case," I said, when we had got outside. "The Chinaman did it."

"You're smart! I got enough now to make out a report."

"What are you going to report?" I asked.

"No clue."

I didn't see him till next day.

"Well," he said, "I got who this Marlind was now, anyway. His business got wiped out and his wife and daughter got killed in an accident, so he stopped taking interest and was just living till he died. He had some bonds left and he lived on the interest. If he had money he didn't clip the coupons. The day he died he clipped 'em for four months—about a thousand dollars."

"And told the Chinaman," I said.

"Told somebody, all right."

We went out to the boatbuilders'.

"You stay outside," O'Malley directed, "and I'll go in and move around, and you tell me when you can't see me."

He went in, and I watched him and then went in afterward.

"When you were in this corner by the door," I said, "I couldn't see you."

"Get me a bucket of water," O'Malley directed.

"What's the idea?" the big man demanded; but he brought the water.

O'Malley emptied it on the floor at the point where I had been unable to see him; and the water spread out over the uneven, cracked concrete and then gathered into several small puddles and one larger one. O'Malley mopped up the large one and then dug the dirt out of the cracks in the concrete where the water had been and put the dirt in an envelope.

"What's that for?" the big man demanded.

"Not a thing."

The little man said nothing, but he watched intently.

"Now what?" I inquired, after we had left the place.

"That's all," O'Malley answered.

We went to the station house and O'Malley gave the envelope with the dirt to an officer, who went away with it. We waited four hours. Then two plainclothesmen came in, bringing the little red-headed man with them.

"Where'd you get him?" O'Malley inquired.

"Grand Central. He'd bought a ticket to Montreal."

"Find anything on him?"

"We ain't searched him yet, but he ain't thrown anything away."

They searched him and produced Marlind's coupons.

"This seems to have been smart work, O'Malley," I said. "I thought it was the Chinaman."

"The Chink never tied them knots," he answered. "Some guy used to boats did. So I was looking for someone on the river all along."

"But what had the pail of water to do with it?"

"This Marlind wasn't killed at night; he stayed home nights. But he was put into the river at night, or the guy would have been seen. If he was killed in the shop he was kept there till dark. He'd been stabbed several times and the shop was all cleaned up; they don't keep those places clean like that. I poured the water where I thought his body must have laid, and the water puddled in the spots where the blood must have puddled. That didn't mean a thing to the big guy; he wasn't in on it. But the red-head guy, who'd seen the blood there, knew what it meant. The red-head, I figure, killed him just before closing time when he and Marlind were alone there. If we'd searched him then we wouldn't have found nothing; but when he started to light out he took the coupons with him. I wasn't even sure either of them had done it, or that the chemist would find blood in the dirt out of the cracks, but now I know he will."

"You'll be promoted for this, O'Malley."

"Say! Listen: I'll be lucky if, after these other cops get through making out their reports, anybody knows I was even on the case."

THE RING

Originally published in *Collier's*, December 13, 1930.

"This is a case," said O'Malley, "where a guy was taken for a ride. He was on the front seat of whatever kind of car they were in and somebody on the back seat shot him in the back of the head and they pushed him out in Morningside Park. We don't know who he was and we don't know who they were and we ain't going to be able to find out; but we got to go and look at where they found him. This is the place."

We got out and looked at it.

"Nobody knows this guy," O'Malley said, "so he probably come from some-wheres else. Everything had been taken out of his pockets and there ain't a label or a laundry mark that could be traced. How you going to solve a case like that?"

He picked up a brightly colored scrap of paper out of the grass; then he picked up a second, then a third and fourth. The scraps said "Square. 40c." and bore serial numbers.

"Here's more trouble," he observed.

"Why?" I asked. "Those are only the halves of motion picture theater tickets that the customers keep. Anybody might have thrown them away."

"Sure. Probably anybody did. But it's all we've got. If I was goin' through a guy's clothes and found those I'd be likely to throw 'em away as not meaning nothing. There's a hundred squares in this town and every one of 'em has got a picture house named after it; and we don't even know it was this town. There's plenty others. Well, we got to go and ask. He was found in Manhattan, so we'll start in Brooklyn; if he'd been found in Brooklyn we'd do the other way about."

We drove to Brooklyn. The sixth picture theater identified the tickets.

"You couldn't remember who bought those tickets, sister?" O'Malley asked.

"Not a chance," the young woman told him.

"But you can tell when they were used?"

"Sure," the young woman assented. "Last night. The numbers show that."

* * * *

"Well, nothing in that," O'Malley said, as we were driving back. "It didn't lead nowhere. So we're back where we started and we'll have to try something else. I'm going to call the office."

He went into a telephone booth and I waited till he came out again.

"They got the guy identified," he stated. "He came from Buffalo. He had a roll of money on him and was going to Paris. His baggage is at the pier and he didn't show up. He didn't know anybody in New York, so it probably was like this: He met some fellows he'd never seen before and they saw his roll and said, 'Let's go to such and such a place and have some fun.' He said all right; but Morningside Park was where he stopped. How you going to find out who they were? You can't. Well, I got to go to a newspaper office and put in an ad."

We stopped at a newspaper office and O'Malley wrote his ad. It read:

"Found. In —— Square picture theater Thursday night. Diamond ring with engraved motto. Valuable. Owner phone Bryant 0001 for appointment."

It was my telephone number.

"What's this about a ring?" I asked.

"This here's the ring."

He gave it to me. It was a big white diamond and inside the gold band was engraved "*Fide, sed cui vide.*"

"That's a fine ring," I said. "It must be worth several thousand dollars. And it's a wise motto: 'Trust, but be careful whom.' But what's all this got to do with this business? Was it the dead man's ring?"

"It was on him."

"But what's the idea of saying you found it in the theater? Who do you expect is going to answer the ad?"

"Listen," O'Malley said. "What you don't know you won't be thinking about. If I told you who might answer the ad, maybe you wouldn't be so useful to me. All you got to do if someone calls you about the ring is say you found it under your seat in the theater; at first you was going to turn it in at the theater office, but then you saw it was valuable and decided to advertise it."

* * * *

The next morning the ad appeared in several newspapers. In the afternoon a voice called up and, an hour later, the speaker appeared at my apartment. He was a short man, heavy set and dark. He looked steadily at me.

"You got the ring?" he asked.

"I have. Can you describe it?"

"Sure. It says inside of it, 'Fid sed q vid.'"

"That's right," I confirmed.

I gave the ring to him and he took a roll of money from his pocket.

"I don't want anything," I told him.

"You're a square bird, but if you live to be a thousand years old you'll never have a nickel."

He went out and I went to the window to look down and watch. He got into a car across the street and drove away. So I called up O'Malley.

"Are you asleep?" I asked him. "Why weren't you on the job here? A man came and claimed the ring and I gave it to him and he's gone away."

"What are you trying to do now?" he asked—"be a detective?"

The next day he called me.

I met him and we drove to Brooklyn. It was a dismal street of once fine houses. There were men in citizens' clothes about, but anyone who didn't know they were cops would better go and live somewhere else. Four of them went up with us to the second floor and there they broke down a door. There were three men inside, and one of them was the man who had claimed the ring. They didn't fight because the cops had the drop on them.

* * * *

"Now maybe you'll tell me what all this means," I said to O'Malley, after they had departed in the wagon. "Of course you had the man who came for the ring followed, and he led you to the others."

"Sure. It was the way I guessed all along. The dead guy met these three guys and they saw his roll and got friendly with him and got him to go along with them."

"I don't mean that," I said. "I mean the ring."

"Oh, the ring was under the dead guy's armpit. When one of 'em dragged him out of the car with his hands under the guy's arms, his ring come off and stayed there. The ring had been stolen a year ago in a jewel robbery. I figured it was worth enough so that, if he knew where he lost it, he'd have taken the chance of going back to look for it. So he didn't know where he'd lost it and, if they'd been to the picture theater and he saw the ad, he'd think he lost it there. I couldn't tell you that because when he come to see you he was looking for a plant. If things looked suspicious he'd say it wasn't the ring he'd lost; or it might be even that he'd bump you off."

"Much obliged," I said sarcastically, "for permitting me to take that risk."

"There wasn't no real risk," he said, "the way you'd do it."

"It was smart police work, O'Malley. You've the right to feel proud of it! And I'm pleased you realized that I would do it as it ought to be done."

"Sure," he answered. "The guy wouldn't suspect nothing as long as you looked dumb, and I figured you'd do that."

THE SLEEPTALKER

Originally published in *Collier's*, April 18, 1931.

"What we got now," O'Malley said, "is a gunman-killing. The guy that got the lead handed him was named Roscoe. He was alone in his apartment and two guys called on him. He let 'em in and they talked for a while and then they pushed him full of bullets. He lived for a few hours but he wouldn't tell who done it. The trouble with this kind of case is that if somebody even saw it done you haven't got any witnesses, and you can't blame people for not talking. If they tell anything, they get locked up and bothered by the cops, and later on they probably get shoved off by the other parties."

"What have they done about the case?" I asked.

"What do they always do? They had about twenty guys that they thought might have done it in the station-house and worked all the old gags on 'em, telling each one his pal had confessed and he'd better come clean and make it easier for himself. But these babies only laughed at 'em. They know there ain't nobody going to confess. So they had to let 'em go. They held one guy."

We stopped in front of the apartment. It was in a good building and was well furnished. The gunman had died in his living-room and there were a couple of bullet holes in the wall to show where they had missed. There were women's things about and an officer was on guard there.

"It was done like this," the officer informed us: "Two birds came here and didn't take the elevator but walked upstairs, so the elevator boy didn't see 'em. He heard the shots and went and got the janitor, and while him and the janitor were coming up in the elevator the two birds walked down again. We know there were two because there were two kinds of bullets in him. Besides, a woman across the street heard the shots and looked out her window and saw 'em walk away. But she was too far off to tell what they looked like."

I looked around the apartment. "This Roscoe and his wife lived pretty well," I commented.

"She wasn't his wife," O'Malley stated. "He's got another place that his wife lives in. These birds have to do their living fast because they don't know how much time they got left for doing it. The girl wasn't here when he got killed."

There was a doll on the girl's dresser.

"It's funny," I said, "how girls that live this way like dolls."

"Sure, they do; but this ain't her doll," O'Malley decided. "They like dolls but they don't play with 'em, but this is a kid's doll because it's been played with un-til it got wore out and had to be mended."

He was right; the doll had a new foot and a new hand. It was neatly dressed in a carefully made checkered dress and it had red hair.

"How about this doll?" O'Malley asked the officer. "Was it just here like this?"

"No; it was wrapped in paper. The plainclothes guys that were here ahead of you unwrapped it to see what it was. The paper and string are in the wastebasket."

* * * *

We went and looked at them. It was ordinary wrapping paper without marks, and ordinary string; it would not be possible to identify them.

"Everything in this place," O'Malley decided, "is the way you'd expect it to be except the doll. You wouldn't expect to find that kind of doll here, so that's what we'd better think about."

"Where are you going?" I inquired of him.

"Over to the station-house and see which of the guys that they've been questioning have families."

We went to the station-house and looked over the list of those who had been questioned and O'Malley checked off the family men. Then we went around to all their homes. At each of them O'Malley asked the women the same rather pointless questions as to where their husbands had been on the afternoon Roscoe was killed; and the women either did not know or gave the same alibis that their husbands had already given. The sixth place we went was the home of Eddie Sunday. His wife, a rather pretty woman with unreadable eyes, said her husband had been home all that afternoon.

"Well," O'Malley said, after we had come out again, "we got a lead now, anyway."

"What do you mean?" I asked. "She told the same story that her husband had already told the officers. I didn't hear anything that would give us a lead."

"Or you didn't see anything?"

"No."

"If you're as dumb as that, I might as well not tell you. We'll go and get the doll."

We went and got the doll and came back to the corner near where Sunday lived. The street was full of children. O'Malley took the doll from its wrapping and held it in his hand, and we walked all along the block but nothing happened. We walked back but still there was nothing; but the third time we did it, a little girl about five years old ran after us.

"You got Mildred," she said accusingly. It was evident that Mildred was the doll.

"Sure," O'Malley answered, "we got your doll and she's got a new hand and a new foot. I'll see you get her back but not right now. Who took her to get her fixed for you? Your papa?"

She shook her head violently. "Uncle Joe."

"That would be Joe Klebo," O'Malley observed to me. "This is Eddie Sunday's kid. Klebo ain't her uncle but she calls him that like kids do a friend of the family. Well, that cheeks up. The guy they're holding is Mike Marla and all they got on him is that Roscoe owed him money that he couldn't collect; but Mike and Joe Klebo are as close together as two fingers on one hand."

"I see how you figure it," I said. "You think that Klebo went and got the doll to take back to the little girl before he and Marla went to see Roscoe. After the shooting, he forgot the package and left it there. But I don't see that that proves anything. He might have been to see Roscoe and left the doll there any time before the shooting happened."

"No; it don't prove nothing," O'Malley assented, "but it all helps. We'll go and talk to Marla."

We went back to the station-house. The gunman was asleep and was talking in his sleep but he did not say anything intelligible. O'Malley awoke him and accused him of committing the killing in company with Klebo, but Marla merely grinned at him.

"I didn't think you'd wake him up, O'Malley," I said, after we had left him. "I thought you'd listen to see if he didn't say something about the shooting."

"A guy don't generally tell anything in his sleep that he wouldn't be willing to tell if he was awake."

"Don't he?" I said surprised. "I didn't know that."

"If you didn't know it, maybe Mike and Joe don't know it either. You had an idea there, even if you didn't know it."

We went into the captain's office and the captain sent two men out to bring in Joe Klebo, and O'Malley went to the captain's desk and began to write something. After he finished he read it over and then handed it to me.

"Does that read like Mike might have said it?" he asked. "You know more about that sort of thing than me."

I read it over.

"I understand," I said. "This is supposed to be something that Mike was saying in his sleep before we woke him up, when we went in there just now. It sounds authentic enough to me; as though he might have said it."

"That's a good word—authentic."

We waited an hour and the two officers brought in Joe Klebo.

"We got the goods on you, Joe," O'Malley told him. "You and Mike Marla done that Roscoe killing and Mike spilt on you."

Joe Klebo grinned at us derisively.

"That's old stuff," he commented. "You dumb cops are always trying them games on us poor boys; but Mike didn't tell nothing on me because he ain't got nothing to tell, and if he did have he wouldn't tell it."

"He told it, all right," O'Malley countered, "but he don't yet know he done it. You'd ought to have more sense, Joe, than to take a sleeptalker along with you when you pull a job."

"Better have Mike in too," the captain suggested.

An officer went and got Mike Marla and Mike grinned at Joe but Joe did not return the grin. His nostrils were white.

"You did some talking just now, Mike," O'Malley told him, "that you don't know about. I'll read it to you."

He went to the captain's desk and got what he had written.

"'Come on, Joe,'" he read, "'we'll get this money or else this guy won't ever have a chance to hold out on us again. . . . Better go up the stairs. . . . Hello, Roscoe, we come to get that jack. . . . What if you ain't got it? You can telephone and get it, can't you? We'll wait till you do. . . . We waited about long enough, Roscoe. How about it? . . . Let him have it, Joe. . . . Well, we both hit him. I guess nobody seen us come out either.'"

Mike Marla was white. It was plain he did not know whether he had said this in his sleep or not. Joe Klebo made a rush toward him but the officers grabbed him.

"I'd knock you off, you rat," Joe yelled at Mike, "if I had anything to do it with!"

"Honest, Joe," Mike whined, "I didn't know I said it. I didn't go to tell anything."

* * * *

"That was sharp police work, O'Malley," I congratulated him after we had left the station-house. "But there's one thing I don't yet understand: When we went to see Mrs. Sunday she didn't tell us anything and yet you said she'd given you a lead. How did she do that?"

"You ain't exactly dumb," O'Malley decided. "It's just that you ain't observing. You didn't notice, when we saw Mrs. Sunday, that the dress she had on was made of the same stuff as the doll was dressed in. She'd made the doll clothes out of the pieces that were left when she made her dress."

FINGERPRINTS

Originally published in *Collier's*, May 9, 1932.

"This is a case," said O'Malley, "where they thought a girl had been hit by an automobile, but when they come to look her over a few times they found that she'd been shot. They don't know who she is or where she come from, and there's some good men working on the case but they ain't found out nothing. Now there'll be one more good man, because I got to go and look at her, but I don't expect to find out any more than they have."

We went and looked at her. She was a very pretty girl and she had been shot twice in the back of the head. They had her clothes at the station house and we looked them over carefully. There were no marks of any kind on any of them. The manufacturer's name in her shoes could not be read and the makers' labels had been carefully cut out of her hat and the fur coat she wore.

"These people that get knocked off," O'Malley stated, "seem to try to make it hard for us. It looks like she cut those labels out herself."

"We got another thing," the desk sergeant offered. "We got a traveling-bag full of clothes that got picked up out of a ditch about a half-mile from where they found this lady. It might not be hers."

"But then again it might," O'Malley answered. "People don't generally throw away full traveling bags without" some reason."

We examined that too. There were no initials on the bag or on the toilet articles it contained and there was no marking on the clothes. We took the clothes out of the bag and compared them with the ones she had had on and it seemed that they ought to fit the same person.

"All this ain't natural," O'Malley concluded. "A woman carries more things than this in a suitcase. She carries letters and most always photographs. Where's her other glove?"

"She didn't have but one," the sergeant answered.

"A woman wears two gloves."

"This one didn't."

"That's a man's glove, O'Malley," I objected, "not a woman's."

"Sure, it's a man's glove and one time it was cleaned, but she might wear man's gloves if she was driving. She have it on?" he asked the sergeant.

"No; it was found near her."

We went back into the outer office of the station.

"So you got nothing more than that?" O'Malley asked.

"Well, we might have one more thing," the sergeant answered. "A guy was driving along the road last night where she was found and he saw a parked car and heard a man and woman quarreling; so this rubberneck stopped his car to listen. When they seen him the quarreling stopped. He couldn't see 'em; it was dark. So he drove on; but before he done that he wrote down the number of the car. He was the kind of guy that would. He called us up just now and gave us the number and they're looking up who the car belongs to. It might not have anything to do with this."

"Probably not," O'Malley decided.

We went out and got back into our car and drove out to where the woman was found, and then on farther to where they found the suitcase, and we looked everywhere along the road to find the other glove, but didn't find it. So O'Malley went into a house and called the station.

"They found who owned that car yet?" he inquired.

"Sure," the sergeant answered. "The name's Norman." He gave us the address. "They've gone over there now," he added.

We were in the Bronx, but now we drove back to Manhattan. It was one of a row of apartment houses very much alike, which had garages behind them. There were police officers all over the place. "They got anything new on this?" O'Malley asked one of the officers.

"Certainly. We got it all solved. This Norman, he's her husband, done it. We found him in bed asleep in the middle of the afternoon and his car has been parked since morning in front of his garage and there's blood in it."

We went behind the house to where they were working on the car. They were powdering it for fingerprints.

"Getting anything?" O'Malley asked them.

"You bet. Two kinds, on the doors and on the windshield—hers and another kind that must be her husband's. Nobody else's."

"Anything on the steering wheel?" O'Malley asked.

"Nothing on the wheel. Those are smeared so they can't be read."

We looked into the car.

"She wasn't driving," O'Malley decided. "There's blood on the right-hand seat but none on the driving seat."

"That was a man's right-hand glove, O'Malley," I insisted.

"Sure. And a man takes off his glove before he pulls a trigger."

We searched the car thoroughly for the other glove, but didn't find it, and then we went up to the apartment. The police had finished questioning Norman but had not taken him to the station house. He was a good-looking young man who sat staring straight before him, paying no attention to anything that went on.

"What's his story?" O'Malley asked the officer in charge of him.

"Says he was in Boston and got home this morning. His wife wasn't here but he didn't think nothing about that because it was morning. Don't know if the car was here then or not, because he was tired and went right to bed."

"Say," O'Malley said to Norman, "you got a pair of brown gloves with yellow stitching?"

"Sure. In the dresser drawer."

We looked in the dresser drawer. There were several pairs of gloves there, but none like the one that had been found, and there was no odd glove.

"Well," O'Malley said, "I guess that's all we can do here."

We went out and got into the car.

"What do you make of it, O'Malley?" I asked. "Is Norman guilty?"

"How do I know?" O'Malley answered.

"Well," I said, "I'd like to stick around."

"I ain't going to do anything more right now. I'll let you know."

The second day afterward he called me up.

"There's something might be going to happen over at the station house," he stated, "if you'd care to be there."

I knew that they had Norman at the station house. I went. There were several people at the station but Norman was not among them, and O'Malley was not there but he was expected. He came in presently, carrying a package, and had a stranger with him.

"This here is Mr. Colling," he introduced him. "Mr. Colling and his wife live in the building next to where Norman lived. So I asked him would he come over to the station house and tell us what he can about the Normans, and he said he would."

We all went into the captain's office.

"The first thing we want you to do, Mr. Colling," O'Malley told him, "is to try on this glove."

He brought out the glove. Colling looked at him quickly in surprise, but he took the glove and put it on. It fitted.

"I don't know anything about this glove," he remarked, "but it would fit a hundred thousand men besides me."

"Sure," O'Malley replied. "Probably it would fit several million. Now the next thing, will you make the fingerprints of your right hand on a piece of paper for this gentleman?"

Colling, frightened, was ready to refuse but saw that it was useless. The expert took his fingerprints. O'Malley unwrapped his parcel and I saw that it was the steering wheel of the Norman car, which had been so wrapped as to preserve its surface. He gave it to the expert, who powdered it with a white powder, and when the powder was blown off, the prints of a man's fingers grasping the wheel remained. The expert compared the prints on the wheel with those of Colling's fingers. Colling, anxious, grew steadily paler.

"They the same?" O'Malley asked the expert, finally.

"Yes."

"Well, Mr. Colling," O'Malley said, "I guess we got you. You'll understand that if I tell you how I done it. This glove here had been cleaned so there was a number inside it like the cleaners always put there. It took me about a day going from one cleaner to another to find out whose mark that was, and then I was lucky because they had it on the books that the gloves had been delivered to your address.

"I asked around and found out that sometimes, when Norman was away, you and Mrs. Norman had been seen together. Norman was out of town a good deal. I asked him, did he have any money, and he said he had about fifteen hundred dollars that his wife kept for him in a savings account, but the bank told me that Mrs. Norman had drawn that money all out the day that she was killed. So then I remembered that she had taken the labels out of her clothes, and there I had it; you and her were going away together, but instead you killed her. You took off your glove before you shot her and afterward you couldn't find it. Then you drove the car home and parked it by the Norman garage as the safest way of getting rid of it."

Colling stared at him; then he broke.

"I had to do it," he said, sobbing. "We had been going together for a year and she said that if I didn't go away with her she'd tell my wife about us."

"I don't understand this, O'Malley," I said, after we had left the station house. "They said there were no prints on the steering wheel and yet you found Colling's prints there."

"Did you fall for that the same as he did?" O'Malley asked. "You ought to try to be smarter. Those weren't his fingerprints. They were mine. I put them on the steering wheel and fixed it with the expert to take a long while examining them while Colling watched him and say that they were his. If he was innocent he'd know it was a plant, but if he was guilty he'd know they might be his. I figured he'd been worrying about losing the glove, and the prints might break him. They did."

"It was great police work," I commented, "and you'll get pleasure out of telling Norman that you've caught the man that did it."

"Me tell him?" O'Malley questioned. "No; I like that guy Norman. He loved his wife. Some harder cop than me'll have to tell him that she had been fooling him for over a year and had taken his money and was leaving him for someone else."

THE FOURTH DEGREE

Originally published in *Collier's*, May 23, 1932.

"What a great break they give a guy when he is a cop!" O'Malley said sarcastically. "Look what kind of a case they give me now! In this case a guy got murdered for the money he was carrying. He come from Philadelphia to New York to collect money that was owing him and afterward he went out to Coney Island and the next morning they found what was left of him in a marsh behind some bushes. They think they got an idea who bumped him but they been working on this case a month and they can't prove nothing. So now they give the case to me to prove what they ain't able to. Is that giving a cop a break?"

"Who is it they suspect?" I asked.

"A guy named Murphy. He was seen getting acquainted with this fellow. They had Murphy in and sweated him a couple of times but they couldn't get nothing on him and so they had to let him go. So now the Chief says to me, 'Go out and get this bird, O'Malley; these cops are dumb!' 'Would somebody that wasn't dumb *be* a cop? I asked him. Well, here we are."

We were, in fact, at Coney Island. We parked the car and got out and walked along a street of amusements.

"This here's the place where he hangs out," O'Malley stated. "I never seen this Murphy, so I got it fixed with an entertainer in the place to introduce me to him."

It was an open-faced café. We went in. It was afternoon but people were dancing and a hard-faced young man sat at a table with a girl in entertainer's costume. I knew by the look in the girl's eyes when she caught sight of us that this was the right man. He was a tough customer. O'Malley surprised me; the moment we entered the place he stopped looking like a cop and looked as hard as Murphy did. I could not tell how he did it. He spoke to the girl and introduced me to her and she introduced us to Murphy.

"These boys are all right," she told him. "The big guy is from my home town."

We sat down and had some beer which they said was near, but it wasn't, and O'Malley and the girl talked about people and a town I'd never heard of. I decided that the place and people were fictitious and that they were getting enjoyment out of their performance. When O'Malley paid for the beer he took out a roll of money and I saw Murphy eying it.

"What have youse guys got in mind?" Murphy asked us.

"When I come to this place," O'Malley stated, "I take in everything."

We got up to go and Murphy got up with us.

"Anything youse want to see," he said, "I can show you. I know the places."

I could see that Murphy followed money when he saw it. He might not intend to steal it, but there was always a chance that some of it might come his way. We went around, three together, and bet on our skill manipulating mechanical race horses and ringing canes and shooting at targets, and Murphy won a couple of dollars.

"This is kind of dull," O'Malley said finally. "Let's find something better. What I want most is to get my fortune told."

We looked at the outside of several fortune-telling places but O'Malley didn't like the looks of them; finally we all three went into one. There was a quite pretty woman inside who told fortunes by looking into a crystal. O'Malley paid her and she looked into the crystal and told him the usual sort of things; he would see some hard times, she said, but in the end he was going to be rich, but he had to watch out for a dark man who was threatening him.

"That's fine," O'Malley told her, "but anybody could tell me those things. How do I know they're true? You tell me something about myself that I know is true and I'll believe you."

The girl looked into the crystal for a while. "You wouldn't want to hear it."

"Sure, I want to," O'Malley said. "Go ahead and tell it, sister."

"No," she refused.

"Go on; I ain't got anything in *my* life to conceal."

"No; you won't like it," she repeated; but he urged her to tell us what she saw. "I see jewels," the girl said. "Diamonds. There's blood on 'em. You and another man—" She stopped and looked at me. "You and this man with you"—she pointed at me—"killed a woman in a hotel room for her jewelry."

"That's a lie!" O'Malley yelled at her. He was very angry. "You got no business telling a customer anything like that. It ain't true and I got a mind to go and complain about you to the police."

"You made me tell it," she answered. "I didn't want to—and I ain't afraid of you going to any cops."

When we got outside, O'Malley stopped and looked back at the place in indecision.

"What do you know about that?" he said to me. "That's a hot one! How did she know about us killing that dame? Did she see it in the crystal or how was it? What we'd ought to do is go back and knock that girl off before she tells anyone. What do you think?"

Till now I hadn't said anything because I couldn't make out what was going on, but now I saw I had to. "I don't think she'll tell anyone," I said. "It's part of her business not to."

"Well, maybe," O'Malley answered doubtfully. "Anyway, she's the only one that knows it." Then he stopped as if he'd recollected and looked at Murphy.

"Youse don't think I'd say anything, do you?" said Murphy. "I'm a right guy. I wouldn't tell no one."

He looked as if he regarded us as dangerous company and would like to get away. We walked on a ways together until we came to a street corner.

"Well," Murphy said, "I guess I got to leave you. I got a date with a friend of mine."

"We'll go with you," O'Malley replied suspiciously. "Is the friend you're going to see a cop?"

Murphy was uneasy. "You got me wrong," he said. "I wouldn't rat on anybody."

"I'd feel better about you," O'Malley told him, "if she hadn't said a dark man was threatening me. You're dark, and I don't know nothing about you except that a girl I'd met introduced you."

We went on and Murphy didn't turn in anywhere. When we came to the end of the street we went down and sat on the beach. There were a good many people on the beach but nobody near us.

"You know what I heard?" O'Malley said to me.

I did not, as usual, know what to say and merely waited

"I heard," O'Malley said, "that there's a current here. You put a body into this water here and it goes out to sea and no one ever finds it."

Murphy was more uneasy still. We sat a while looking at the ocean. Then O'Malley took out his gun, unloaded it, snapped it to be sure it was working right, reloaded it and put it away. Murphy watched him.

"It'll be dark now pretty quick," O'Malley told me.

"Say!" Murphy exploded. "I know what youse two guys are thinking. You're thinking you'll knock me off for fear I'll tell the cops. But you got me wrong, I tell you. Youse two fellows ain't the only ones that ever shoved anybody off. I done it myself about a month ago."

"Anybody could say that," O'Malley told him unbelievingly.

"It's right, though. Didn't you see it in the papers? A guy from Philadelphia."

"I didn't see it," O'Malley said.

"Didn't you either?" Murphy asked me anxiously. I shook my head.

"I done it, though," he asserted. "I met this guy in a café and saw he had a roll on him and so I stuck around with him. When he got ready to go I told him I had a car and would drive him in. I swiped a car belonging to a friend of mine and when we got part way I bumped him on the head and took his pocketbook that had his roll in it and hid him in some bushes."

"What do you think of it?" O'Malley asked me.

I wondered what he might want me to say. "It might be true," I ventured; but O'Malley shook his head incredulously.

"Sure, it's true," Murphy insisted. "You got a car here? If you don't believe me, I'll show you where I done it."

We went and got the car and Murphy directed us as we drove back toward New York. Part way in, he stopped us.

"Right here," he said, "is where I bumped him and over there is where I put him in the bushes."

We got out and looked at the place. There were footmarks in the soft ground, but there was nothing else, and after studying it O'Malley turned to Murphy unbelievingly.

"That's what *you* say," he observed.

"Sure I do. Now listen. After I hid the guy I drove on a ways, then I looked at the pocketbook. I seen it had his initials on it, so I took the money out and stuck the book in some weeds beside a culvert right over there."

* * * *

We got back in the car and drove a little farther. Murphy got out. He fumbled in some weeds and came back bringing the pocketbook.

"There!" he said triumphantly. "Am I a right guy or am I yellow? Youse don't think now, do you, that I'd talk to cops?"

"Sure, I do," O'Malley answered. "You're talking to one now."

He put the handcuffs on him.

21

"This is great work, O'Malley!" I said admiringly. "You certainly gave him the fourth degree—outguessed him! I see through it now. Of course you had the fortune-teller fixed to say what she did."

"You're getting clever."

"You say cops are dumb, hut they're not all dumb—not while you're one of them."

"Sure, we're dumb," he answered. "The only advantage we got is that birds like our pal Murphy here are still dumber than we are."

IN A MIRROR

Originally published in *Collier's*, July 9, 1932.

"This is a Long Island murder," said O'Malley, "so whoever gets credit out of it, it won't be me; but they got me working on the Manhattan end of it. Am I a messenger-boy or what am I? These were two New York girls that lived together, and for a joke they put an ad in a paper like it was some girl that wanted to get married. Well, a lot of guys answered it and they liked one letter pretty well, so they wrote back to him and met the guy.

"These girls were secretaries, but one of 'em, named Miss Wells, had some dough she had inherited from her father. Then she fell in love with the guy that answered the ad and agreed to marry him; so she took four thousand dollars out of the bank and went out on Long Island with him to buy a house he'd showed her there. They found her murdered."

"I suppose," I said, "as long as girls consent to marry men whom they know nothing about, such murders will happen."

"Does a girl ever know anything about a guy, even if she's married to him?" O'Malley answered. "This guy gave the girl a false name but now we got his right one. This is him."

He took a police flier from his pocket, with the usual portrait and the heading, "Wanted for Murder," and I studied it.

"He looks capable of any crime," I decided.

"Yeah? You think that because he's wanted for murder. If he'd just gave some money to a hospital you'd think he had a fine face. This guy was raised in Manhattan and they think he's hiding here, so I got to trace him down, But first I got to find out where to look for him."

We drove out onto Long Island to where they had the girl. She was an unusually pretty girl and was about twenty-two years old. They had her clothes there and the things she had been carrying; and there was a faded bunch of sweet peas which had been fresh when she was wearing them and her handbag, which the money had been in, was still open as it had been found.

"He probably bought those flowers for her," I hazarded, "and she thanked him and pinned them on and maybe kissed him for them, and all the time he knew what he was going to do to her."

"Say, you're a great guy to go around with, ain't you?" O'Malley remarked sarcastically. "When you get thoughts like that why don't you keep 'em to yourself?"

He examined all the articles very carefully.

"They got this guy's ma and pa here," he told me. "He lived with 'em. That's why I had to come out here to talk with 'em. But do I like the job? I'll say not. Auston their name is."

But I had already seen the name James Auston on the police flier. We went to the station house. They had the girl she had lived with there and had been questioning her, and in another room they had the young man's parents. They were a neat, respectable couple, a small middle-aged man and a little gray-haired woman, who looked as though events had stunned them.

"I guess you seen enough cops already," O'Malley told them, "but there's still some questions that I got to ask you. I want to know who your son's friends was and what places he most often went to."

We sat down and the little man gave us a list of people and places which O'Malley noted down. The woman listened. Her eyes were red with weeping. When we got up to go, she rose and faced us.

"He didn't do it!" she said, trying to keep steady. "I want you to understand that. I realize, of course, that you don't know anything about him; but I'm his mother and have known him all his life and I tell you he didn't do it!"

She couldn't say any more than that because at that point she began to weep again. O'Malley looked very uncomfortable.

"Yes, ma'am," he evaded her.

I was glad when we got out of there.

"That's the trouble with it," I complained. "Back of the criminal are innocent people—"

"Sure," O'Malley interrupted. "Do you think you can do something about that? Well, I got his friends' names that I came out here for, so what I'd ought to do now is go back to Manhattan and question those people; but it ain't likely he can get away, and that old lady has given me an interest in this case I didn't have before. Let's go and look at the scene of this homicide."

"Where was she killed?" I asked.

"Right there in the house that she thought they were going to buy to live in, with the piece of pipe you seen there in the station house. Some plumber had left it lying handy for him, or else he'd put it there himself to serve his purpose. Let's go."

* * * *

We drove to the house, which was in a new real estate development. There were rows of these small houses, all alike, for sale mostly to young married couples. Some were already occupied; others finished but vacant, with "For Sale" signs on them; others were only partly completed, with men still working. Around them were the truck gardens that once had filled the neighborhood and close by were greenhouses.

We had no trouble picking the right house; there were parked cars and people staring at it, and a uniformed officer on the doorstep. There were more cops inside, in plain clothes and uniform; and it was easy to tell the room where it had happened—the freshly laid floor and hardly-dry plaster were stained with dreadful evidence.

"The real estate guy found her," O'Malley stated. "Auston and her had looked at the place several times before and said they'd buy; so this time nobody came with 'em but they just gave 'em the key. When they didn't come back to complete the purchase and the key wasn't returned, the real estate guy came to find out about it. The door was locked but he had another key, and the shades in this room were drawn."

We went all over the house and O'Malley looked in all the rooms, but we learned nothing more than we already knew.

24

"What are you doing here, fellow?" one of the plainclothesmen demanded of O'Malley.

"I'm on this case. I'm supposed to be looking for the guy."

"Well, you don't expect to find him here, do you? He got through his business here. Why don't you work on your own island?"

"I guess you're right, at that," O'Malley admitted. "I got no business here."

* * * *

We went out of the house, but we did not return to Manhattan. Instead, we walked all around the neighborhood and O'Malley examined the surroundings closely. Next to the house was a vacant lot with tall weeds growing in it, and O'Malley picked up among the weeds a small, round piece of glass—a mirror. We went back to the house.

"Did you guys find the girl's vanity?" he asked one of the officers.

"She didn't have none."

"Yeah?" O'Malley said. "You're smart, ain't you? She was out with her beau that she was going to marry, on an all-day excursion, and she didn't have no rouge or even powder with her?"

"We didn't find one, anyway." the officer said, with less assurance.

We went back and looked thoroughly all about in the weeds but we could not find the rest of the vanity. Finally our search brought us to the door of the greenhouse. Inside, a big man with a watering-pot was sprinkling sweet peas. We stood and watched him. Suddenly O'Malley turned around and went back toward the spot where we had found the mirror, and after going a little way he picked up the vanity.

"You've got it now!" I exclaimed.

"Yeah, I guess this was hers, all right; it's got her right initial on it. We couldn't find it before because we didn't know where to look. Gee, this is a funny case!"

"Why is it funny?" I inquired.

"It ain't the way it looks."

He put the vanity in his pocket and we went back to the greenhouse. The gardener, who was a muscular man with a stolid, foreign look, turned and stared at us.

"This place for sale?" O'Malley asked him.

"Don't know. The boss ain't here."

"When'll he be back?"

"Maybe two, three days. Don't know. He been away a week now."

"You tell him a guy was here might buy the place and find out what he says. Meantime, I want to look at it."

The greenhouse had a square room with a brick floor, off of which opened a long, dirt-floored gallery, and from this there opened other galleries. We went into the gallery.

"You got nice flowers here," O'Malley commented to the gardener. But I could see he was not looking at the flowers.

"See if it looks like something was buried here," he told me *sotto voce*.

We went through all the galleries, one by one, inspecting them carefully.

"How about it?" he inquired.

"I didn't see anything suspicious," I replied; but I didn't know what we were looking for. We had come back to the room with the brick floor.

"How about here?" he asked.

"You can't tell here," I said, "because the floor is brick."

"Yeah? Well, there's a way to find it out."

He picked up the watering-pot which the gardener had been using, filled it at the hydrant and began to pour water on the bricks.

"Hey! what you do there?" the gardener shouted at him, but O'Malley paid him no attention. He filled the watering-pot at the hydrant several times till he had wet all the bricks. Then be stood looking at them. In one place small air bubbles were rising through the water between the bricks, but they stopped as the spot got dry. O'Malley picked up a spade, but now the gardener interfered violently.

"You get out of here!" he shouted. "You got no business here. I put you out!" He grabbed O'Malley and tried to push him out of the greenhouse.

"Go and get some of them cops," O'Malley directed me.

I did not know what this was all about, but I went to the house and got the cops; I ran. When we returned O'Malley had the gardener backed against the wall and was dislodging some of the bricks. Two of the cops grabbed the gardener and another one helped with the bricks. When they had taken out quite a lot of bricks O'Malley began to dig, while the rest of us peered excitedly down into the hole. They had dug about four feet when O'Malley straightened.

"Well," he said, "we found the guy they said I was to look for. This guy buried here is Auston. They can tear up their flier calling him a murderer. Put the cuffs on that gardener. We'd ought to find her four thousand dollars somewheres around here—it might be buried in a flowerpot."

* * * *

"Explain this O'Malley," I demanded, when we were again in the car.

"You hadn't ought to need any explaining," he replied. "You seen it all. Everybody had this case wrong because it looked so simple. This gardener, whose name, they say, is Mellin, looks dumb, but he's a smart guy. He had the run of the place because his boss is away. Auston and Miss Wells had come out here a lot of times to look at the house, and probably they'd bought flowers here and the gardener talked with 'em. I guess Auston was in love with her all right. He give her a false name at first because answering the ad was just a joke to him, but I hear from these cops that after he got to know her he give her his right name.

"The day they brought the money out, they may have told the gardener they had it or else he saw it in her handbag. He went up to the house with 'em and he knocked 'em both off. He was a smart guy: he knew that if they found Miss Wells and didn't find Auston. Auston'd be the one suspected and we'd be trying to find him and look for no one else. Maybe he carried Auston's body to the greenhouse covered up with canvas; people were used to seeing him working around the place and wouldn't suspect anything."

"That's all plain enough," I insisted, "but how did you find it out?"

"Why, I was as wrong on this case as anybody when I come out here. Then I found the mirror out of her vanity. Of course it might not be hers; but she wouldn't be out with her beau without one and they hadn't found one with her things. I figured the vanity had been thrown away by Auston and the mirror had fell out of it; but I couldn't find the rest of it because I thought it had been thrown from near the house and was looking in the wrong place. Then we looked into the greenhouse and the gardener was watering sweet peas. I thought, 'Here's where she got her flowers; so maybe the vanity got thrown away from this place.'

"I walked from there toward where we'd found the mirror, and there the rest of the vanity was. But if it had been thrown from the greenhouse maybe it hadn't been thrown by Auston but by someone else. Then what had become of him? Had somebody knocked him off with her? I looked all through the greenhouse to see if there was any sign of ground being disturbed as if Auston had been buried there, but there wasn't. Then I wet down the bricks. When bubbles came up between some of the bricks and that part of the floor got dry much quicker than any other, because the water ran down through the dirt in the cracks, I knew the bricks had been taken up recently and the dirt between 'em was soft.

"It proved to be like I'd said—the gardener grabbed the vanity out of her handbag with the money. When he took the money out of his pocket to hide it in the furnace-room where we found it, he found the vanity with it. He couldn't have that around, so he went to the greenhouse door and threw it away. Even if it was found, he figured, they couldn't connect him with it."

"That was good reasoning," I congratulated him, "and this ought to get you promotion."

"You think so? When them Long Island cops get through telling the newspapers how they caught the guy, you won't know there ever was a cop from Manhattan on their island."

THE WRONG HAT

Originally published in *Collier's*, July 16, 1932.

"If any guy but me had this case." said O'Malley, "he'd make himself a name out of it. I won't because when I get a case like this something unlucky always happens. This is a case of a dead guy riding in a taxicab. Him and some other people took the cab and later the other folks got out and when the taxi-driver got to where he had been told to go he found his passenger had been shot. A lot of other cops are working on the case."

"Haven't they any clue at all?" I asked.

"Yeah, they got one thing. The dead guy's hat don't fit him. They give me the job to find out why it don't; so I got to go and look at this guy, but I don't expect to find out nothing."

We went and looked at him. He was a coarse-looking man of middle age but he appeared well cared for. His hair had just been trimmed and he was freshly shaven and his nails were manicured. All his clothing was brand-new. His linen was new and never had been laundered.

"I'd say," O'Malley remarked, "that this guy was dressed up in a way he wasn't used to."

The hat, however, was not new. We tried it on the dead man and it proved much too large. O'Malley picked a woman's long golden hair off the hat and put it in an envelope.

"They are holding the taxi-driver at headquarters as a witness," he stated. "I guess we got to see him next."

We went and talked with the taxi-driver.

"You tell us, fellow." O'Malley invited, "how all this was."

"Well, mister," said the taxi-driver, "I was cruising along Madison Avenue about two A. M. and I seen three guys standing on the curb with their arms around each other, singing close harmony, and a lady was watching 'em. So I slows up and the lady stops the cab.

"Two of the guys was in evening clothes and had high hats, and the third one was this guy that is now dead. The lady was in evening clothes too. The three guys got into the cab, still singing, with their arms around one another and staggering so that I seen that they were pretty drunk, and the lady got in afterward. The guys sat on the back seat and kept singing, and the lady sat on one of the little front ones.

"I drove to Park Avenue, like they told me, and the lady and one guy got out there. Then I drove to East Seventieth Street and another guy got out. 'Take Mr. Sullivan,' he says, 'to Riverside Drive and One Hundred and Twentieth Street. That's where he lives. He's feeling low now but the drive'll do him good.' So I done that. When I tried to wake him up to find which house it was, I seen that he was dead. So then I took him to the police station. That's all I know about it, mister."

"Didn't you hear the shot?" I asked. "There wasn't no shot fired in my cab. Would I be drivin' a cab and not know what happened in it?"

"Was these folks old or young?" O'Malley asked him.

"They was all young except the dead guy, but I can't describe 'em because where they got in, it wasn't near a street lamp and I couldn't see 'em very good."

"Well. O'Malley," I said, when we had left the driver, "you've got a lead anyway. The man's name was Sullivan and you know the neighborhood where he lived. There was a drunken party and Sullivan got shot. I think it was in the cab. They were all happy when they got into the cab and then there was a drunken quarrel. It is quite possible the driver did not hear the shot; or the last man to leave the cab may have bribed him. Find the last man who left the cab and you'll have Sullivan's murderer."

"Yeah, Sullivan!" O'Malley said. "That's a good name. Or would you think the name might be Heidenbacher and he lived in Brooklyn? They wouldn't give the guy's right name. You ain't ever very smart! Where did the hat come from? If one of the guys in the cab made a mistake and took the wrong hat, this'd be a high hat, wouldn't it? And the medical examiner says the dead guy hadn't had a drink, but he was a drinkin' man, and I don't think none of the others had either."

I was amazed.

"How do you figure it, then?" I asked incredulously.

"I ain't figuring. I got nothing but a hunch. I think the guy was dead before they ever got into the cab. There was some reason they couldn't leave him there in Madison Avenue. They were holding him up as if he was alive and then they seen the cab; so they began to sing and act like they were drunk. . . . All that ain't my present business. I got to take this hat around to all the stores that sell this make of hat and find if anyone remembers selling it."

* * * *

I went around with him to several stores, but we learned nothing and I presently got tired of it. I left him and met him the next day.

"Made any progress?" I inquired.

"I ain't made a step. I been to all the stores and nobody remembers this hat because it was sold too long ago. Now I been going to the restaurants around Madison Avenue and showing it to the hat-check people. Would you believe it, I ain't seen a hat-check girl yet that has gold hair!"

He had the hat in a paper bag. I went along with him. The hat-check girl in the fourth restaurant we visited said quickly:

"Oh, you've got Mr. T. O. Annan's hat. That's good. His butler telephoned yesterday about it and said I'd given him the wrong hat—though I can't see how I did it, because I know his hat."

We went to give Mr. Annan back his hat. It was a fine big house around the corner from Madison Avenue. The butler came to the door and we gave him the hat and he gave us the other one. It was a brand-new hat and the maker's label was stamped in the leather of the sweatband.

I was amused.

"You've traveled a long way, O'Malley," I said, "without getting anywhere. The hats were exchanged in the restaurant. I don't suppose you'll accuse T. O. Annan, who is over seventy years old and one of the richest and most philanthropic men in New York of knowing anything about this murder."

"No—I might be dumb, but I ain't so dumb as that. I'm out of luck, the way I always am."

* * * *

I didn't see him for two days.

"Got anything yet?" I asked him when I met him.

"I have got plenty. This dead guy's name was Klein. The department had his fingerprints but they'd mislaid 'em. He used to be a valet, but now he was a bum and hung out on the Bowery. I thought all along he was a bum in spite of how he was dressed up. I been to the Bowery hotel where he hung out and talked with his friends and now I got to go back to T. O. Annan's, but first I want to call them up."

I waited while he telephoned.

"T. O. ain't home," he said. "I wanted to be sure of that. Annan's got a grandson who's in college, and a granddaughter that lives with him. That's all his family. The young folks' name is Cairn."

"I know that." I told him.

"Yeah, and I guess all the rest of N. Y. knows it too."

We told who we were and asked to see Miss Cairn. She was very pale and frightened and about twenty years old, and she had gold hair.

"You're—the police?" she said.

"That's right," O'Malley told her.

He took three worn and greasy letters from his pocket.

"You look at these," he said, "but you ain't supposed to tear 'em up."

She hardly glanced at them and then began to weep. "You've read them?" she inquired.

"Sure. I had to read 'em because I am a cop. Now don't you think you'd better tell us all about it?"

"I'll have to, now that you've seen these. He shot himself. I know you won't believe it. I don't expect anybody ever to believe it. Of course he didn't mean to. It is all too terrible! Grandfather always thought that Mother was perfect; she was his only daughter and he thinks that she was wonderful and it would almost kill him if he thought that she was not.

"Well, once in her life—just once—she wasn't. This man knew about it and stole the letters which showed she wasn't; and after that she had to pay him so that Grandfather wouldn't know. He would disappear for quite a long while and she would think she was rid of him, and then he would come back and she would have to pay him again. After she died, he came to me. He showed me copies of the letters, but I wouldn't believe him. So then he gave me one of them—there were four letters at first, and he kept three. Then I knew it was true, and I had to pay him so that Grandfather would never know."

"Yeah," said O'Malley, "I thought it might be like that. Tell us the rest of it."

"Last week, after I hadn't seen him for a long while, he came back and wanted a thousand dollars. I didn't have that much money. I gave him two hundred dollars and told him I'd try to get the rest, but I couldn't do that without telling why I needed it. My brother Bob was home from college for the weekend, and finally I had to tell him and ask him if he could get it; and he tried to get it through his room-mate who was here with him, but they couldn't.

30

"I'd always met that man outside the house, but that night I didn't meet him. I knew he wouldn't come here unless I was home, so we stayed out as late as we could. He came as soon as we got home; I guess he'd been watching for us. He was all dressed up in things he'd bought with the money I'd given him and he was very angry because I hadn't met him, and very threatening.

"I wanted to see the man alone, because my brother has a violent temper, but the boys wouldn't let me. When he got violent Bob got violent too. Then the man took a revolver out of his pocket and threatened Bob with it and Bob tried to put him out of the house. Bob had him from behind, pushing him, and the man tried to reach around his own body under his other arm and point the gun at Bob, and it went off and he shot himself."

"I'm listening," O'Malley said.

"We just stood and looked at one another. Then the boys said they would take the man out and leave him in the street and maybe nobody would ever know. So they got one on each side of him and walked with him down the steps as if he were still alive and walked with him along the street; because we were afraid to leave him in front of the house.

"There was a policeman up the street, walking the other way, and so he didn't see us, but I was afraid he would; and then I saw a cab I said to the boys. 'Sing! Sing and act drunk!' So we all acted drunk and got into the cab. We told the driver a number on Park Avenue and John and I got out there; and Bob went on farther, and then he got out too and we all came back here to the house.

"In the morning Grandfather said he didn't have the right hat. He'd put his hat down on the stand when he came home and the servants hadn't put it away. Then the man had put his hat there too, and when we were taking him out of the house I'd picked up the wrong hat. There's a restaurant near here where Grandfather sometimes eats, and he had been there that evening, and I convinced him that the hats must have been changed in the restaurant."

"You know what became of the gun, Miss Cairn?" O'Malley asked her.

"Yes. I have it. We were so excited we forgot all about the gun and when we got back to the house I found it lying on the rug where he had dropped it."

"I want the gun. Don't you go and got it. You just show me where it is."

We followed her upstairs and, in a dresser drawer, hidden among silk underthings, she showed us a cheap nickel-plated revolver. O'Malley picked it up carefully in a handkerchief.

"I don't know how this is coming out, Miss Cairn," he told her, "but I got an idea, if there ain't, no fingerprints on this gun but Klein's and yours, and yours are over his and yours ain't on the trigger, the medical examiner might pronounce this accidental death and that will be the end of it."

* * * *

"Was it the hat that kept you on the right track, O'Malley?" I inquired when we had left the house.

"Sure. Would a guy like T. O. Annan, who was used to wearing a comfortable old hat, put on a brand-new hat a couple of sizes too small for him and walk home without knowing the difference? So the hats must have been changed there in the house. Then they identified this Klein and, remembering how he was dressed, I knew what I might have to look for. I went to the Bowery and picked up the letters where he'd parked 'em with another bum for safety. But can you beat my bad luck? Do I ever get put on a good case but what it blows up on me?"

"You're blowing this case up yourself," I told him. "All you've got to do is make a hint of what we just heard public and your name will be on the front page of every newspaper in New York tomorrow morning."

"But would I sleep at night? It's my bad luck that when I get a swell case, a philanthropic old guy like T. O. Annan and a kid like Miss Cairn get in the works, and I have to keep my mouth shut. Because I was born unlucky."

SOILED DIAMONDS

Originally published in *Collier's*, September 17, 1932.

"What we got now," said O'Malley, "is a jewelry salesman got murdered and robbed. They tell me they got the case as good as solved, but still they put me on it. What good I should go around and ask a lot of questions when they already got the answers? This was a salesman named Alliday and he worked for a jewelry house downtown called Morant & Company. Well, they had to send fifty thousand dollars' worth of diamonds to a jewelry store in the Bronx, so Alliday took 'em in a cab and another guy went with him.

"When they was in Central Park the driver heard a shot fired in his cab and slowed up to find out what was wrong, and the other guy jumped out and run away into the bushes. A lot of people and cars got around, and they got a cop, and the cop went in the taxi with Alliday to the hospital, but by the time they got there the guy was dead."

"Have they got the man who did the shooting?"

"They got one they think is him. Burrel his name is, and he was a friend of Alliday's. They got him at headquarters and the taxi guy, too, who they're holding for a witness."

"Well, what's to be worked on, then," I asked, "if they've already got him?"

"That's what I told you in the first place."

"Did they get back the diamonds?"

"He had got rid of the diamonds and the gun. I got to go and talk with him, but I don't expect he'll tell me anything."

We went to headquarters and saw Burrel. He was an undersized young fellow of unpleasant appearance and had, I thought, a particularly evil face.

"How long had you known Alliday?" O'Malley asked him.

"A couple of months."

"Got acquainted with him, did you, because you knew his business and thought you'd stick him up?"

"I was at a picture show when this thing happened."

"Yeah, I heard you said that. You're out of luck that there don't none of the attendants at the picture theater remember seeing you."

The taxi-driver's name was Durman. He was about twenty-five years old and looked like any other taxi-driver.

"You're sure this Burrel is the guy that was in your cab?" O'Malley asked him.

"He looks like the guy," the taxi-driver answered, "but I never seen him but that one time, so maybe I couldn't really swear to him."

"You tell us about Burrel getting in the cab."

"Why, I was waiting in the cab when Alliday came out of the office building, and this other guy—Burrel, if he's the right one—was standing near the corner. He seen Alliday and came up and spoke to him, and they talked for a minute, friendly, and then both got into the cab. They kept on talking but I didn't pay attention or even hear what they was saying; and in the park I heard the shot."

He described the rest of the event just as O'Malley had already told it to me.

"Say, listen," he said just as we were leaving him, "how long are you guys going to keep me here?"

"I got nothing to do with that," O'Malley told him.

"Well, somebody has. You treat a guy that's just a witness like he had done something. I got a wife, and she's worrying her heart out and the cops are bothering her."

"They got no business to do that," O'Malley said. "I'll see they quit it. You got any message you want I should give your wife?"

"If you see her, tell her to stop worrying."

"Get anything from either of them?" I asked after we had left them.

"Not a thing; and now I got to go and see Morant & Company, and it ain't likely I'll get anything there, either."

We went downtown. Morant & Company's offices were on an upper floor of a tall building, and Morant himself, the senior partner, saw us.

"Anything unusual, Mr. Morant," O'Malley asked, "about the way them diamonds were being sent?"

"Nothing whatever. It was all in accordance with our usual custom. We continually receive requests from jewelers to show them diamonds from which they can make selections, and one of our salesmen takes the diamonds to them in a cab. It was unusual, however, that Alliday took anyone with him. He was supposed to go alone."

"Yeah? Well, this time it seems he didn't. I don't suppose you know what time he left here?"

"We know exactly. We keep a record when stones are sent out and returned. I'll get it for you."

Morant sent for the record. Alliday had left the company's offices a little after three.

"I see," said O'Malley. "So it was this way: Alliday took the diamonds, went down in the elevator to the street and found a cab—"

"Oh, not that way at all," Morant told him. "We don't care to have a salesman with a pocketful of diamonds wandering about the streets looking for a cab. One of the boys went down and got the cab for him."

"I'd like to see that boy."

* * * *

The boy proved to be a frank-faced and intelligent young fellow.

"You see anybody hanging around the building entrance like they was watching for Alliday when you went down to get the cab?" O'Malley asked him.

"I didn't notice anybody in particular. There were plenty of people in the entrance and on the street, of course."

"Tell us how you done it, son."

"Why, the way I always do it. There's a cab stand at the corner and I went and got a cab and came back in it and told the man to wait, and then I came up and told Mr. Alliday it was there, and he went down to it."

"Know the cab-driver?"

"By sight. He's carried salesmen plenty times before."

34

We went down to the street. There was a cigar store in the building entrance and O'Malley went into it and telephoned headquarters.

"What did you tell headquarters?" I inquired of him.

"Told 'em I wasn't learning nothing. Well, here we take a cab."

We went to the cab stand on the corner and got a cab, and O'Malley looked at his watch as we got into it. Then we drove north through the downtown district and along Fifth Avenue and turned into the park.

"Here's where it happened," O'Malley told me finally.

The murderer had picked out an excellent place for it. Bushes on both sides hid the road, and there was less traffic on this road than on most of the park driveways. We got out and spent some time examining the locality, but we didn't find anything. Then we drove to the hospital and, on reaching it, O'Malley again looked at his watch.

"O. K.," he stated. "Alliday left Morant's at three-five o'clock and they got him here, according to the hospital records, at five minutes of four. It's about the same time of day and traffic is about the same, and he done the trip in one minute less than we did, but we might have spent more time in the park."

"What does that show?" I asked.

"Shows the taxi-driver told the truth and didn't go nowhere but where he said he did. That being the case, I guess I'll give his message to his wife."

We drove to Durman's apartment. It was in an unattractive building in the Bronx. A smell of cooking greeted us. Mrs. Durman was in the kitchen, cooking a chop and some potatoes, and a pot of soup was simmering on the stove. She was about twenty-two years old and poorly dressed, but I have never seen a more startlingly beautiful young woman.

"I got a message from your husband," O'Malley told her. "He said to tell you not to worry."

"I'm not worrying. But the police keep coming here and I don't like it because of the neighbors."

"They got no business to. I'll put a stop to it."

He sat down as if he wanted to keep up the conversation and I was amused to see that he was attracted by the woman. They talked for a while.

"You wouldn't want to go to a picture show tonight?" O'Malley asked her bashfully.

"Not with my husband being held."

I was sorry for her, but I felt like laughing at O'Malley.

"Well, O'Malley," I kidded him after we had got outside, "you certainly fell for that woman. She had you going. It's the first time I ever saw you fall for one of them, but I don't blame you. She's a knock-out. Put that girl in the right clothes and the right surroundings and she'd have it over all of them."

"That's right," O'Malley agreed. "But it wouldn't do me no good if I was to fall for her, because she's married to this taxi guy. It's a pity he don't make enough to dress her up."

We parted and I did not see him till the next day.

"Anything new?" I asked him.

"Sure. They found the gun in the park where the guy threw it."

"Fingerprints on it?"

"It had been rained on. They tried to trace it by the number, but it had been stole a month ago from the guy that had a right to own it; so there's no clue."

"You better trace it," I urged, "because it will be the best evidence you can have against Burrel."

"You're smart," O'Malley said.

"How did they connect Burrel with the murder in the first place?" I inquired. "You haven't told me that."

"That was simple. Alliday wouldn't have taken nobody in the cab with him unless he knew him, and this taxi-driver gave a pretty good description of the guy. They looked for who among Alliday's friends answered that description, and Burrel did and couldn't prove where he was when the murder happened."

"They got the right man," I declared. "I knew that when I looked at him. Did you take Mrs. Durman to a picture show?" I asked derisively.

"I went out there but she wouldn't go with me. I'm going out there now."

There was a uniformed policeman in front of Durman's door and Mrs. Durman asked at once the meaning of it.

"I put him there," O'Malley told her, "to keep the other cops away. You ain't been bothered since, have you?"

"No," she replied, "but it makes me wonder what the other tenants in the building think about it."

"I'll have him taken off then."

* * * *

Everything in the place was exactly as it had been the day before. Mrs. Durman was getting her luncheon ready and soup was simmering on the stove.

"You're certainly some cook!" O'Malley told her. "Your soup ain't healthy for a hungry man to smell. It makes him hungrier. You wouldn't let me taste it, would you?"

"I'll give you some," she offered.

"Don't bother. I'll get it myself."

Before she could prevent him he had dipped a ladleful from the bottom of the pot, inspecting it closely. Then he took the kettle from the stove and, following his directions, I helped him strain the soup through a dish-towel, and I saw unset diamonds glistening among the meat and vegetables that were left.

"Were you kidding me into believing that Burrel had done it, O'Malley?" I asked, after we had taken Mrs. Durman to the station-house, "or did you believe it yourself?"

"Sure I believed it," he replied. "The first I thought it might not be that way was when Morant & Company's boy says Durman had drove their salesmen on them trips before; then when I seen Mrs. Durman I got sure of it. You said yourself she'd be a knock-out if she had the clothes; and she knew that a lot better'n you and figured she'd get 'em any way she could.

"Durman knew that when he carried salesmen on them trips they were loaded up with jewels and him and his wife fixed the job up between 'em. After the boy had got Durman's cab and Durman was waiting for Alliday to come down, he went in the cigar store and telephoned his wife, and she went and waited for him in the place they had picked out in the park. Of course there wasn't nobody but Durman and Alliday in the cab. Durman knocked Alliday off. Mrs. Durman was there and he slipped her the diamonds and the gun before the crowd begun to gather.

"Mrs. Durman threw away the gun, so it couldn't be connected with 'em, and Durman took the cop into his cab and beat it for the hospital to tell his story. He's a smart guy, and so he described as the third man in the cab a fellow he'd once seen with Alliday. It was his luck that Burrel didn't have no alibi."

"But what made you think the diamonds were in the soup?"

"Why, there was always the question, if Burrell done the job, whether Durman had been in on it with him; and if he was, Burrel might have took the diamonds out to Durman's place. So they searched Durman's place but they didn't find nothing. I guess Mrs. Durman didn't expect it would be searched and put the diamonds in the soup when the cops came, because it was the quickest and safest place to hide 'em; and afterward she never had a chance to dispose of 'em.

"After I got the hunch Durman might have done the job alone, you and I went out and talked with Mrs. Durman and I looked the place over and I couldn't see nowhere in them two rooms where the stones could have been hidden that the guys searching wouldn't have found 'em. If I could have got her to go to a picture show we'd have searched the place again.

"I went out to her place three different times of day, wondering whereabouts the stones could be, and every time the soup was cooking on the stove. That didn't seem natural."

"You're a clever cop, O'Malley."

"You tell 'em that at headquarters, will you?" he replied. "I've been trying a long time now to get somebody to think that, and I ain't found nobody that will believe me yet."

THE LOCKED DOOR

Originally published in *Collier's*, October 12, 1932.

"You like a case where there ain't nothing to go on," O'Malley said, "and now I got one. This is a case where a guy without no clothes on was found dead in an apartment that ain't occupied by anybody. There don't nobody know who he was and nobody seen him go into the building, so it looks as though we won't find out much about it. Here's the place."

It was a cheap but fairly respectable building on the West Side, renting furnished apartments. Although it was five stories high there was no elevator. We walked up two floors to an apartment in the rear. A uniformed officer was on duty there.

"What about this case?" O'Malley asked him.

"You know as much as me. This guy had no business in the building. He came in here and either somebody came in with him or somebody was waiting for him and bunged him on the head. Then they took the clothes off him and walked out with 'em."

"That seems a strange thing to do," I said. "I suppose it was done to prevent identification."

"You got as good a right to guess as anybody."

There were old bloodstains, but no other evidence that anyone had been there. The windows looked out on a deserted court, and the undisturbed dust on the furniture showed that we would find no fingerprints. Evidently it was a long time since the apartment had been occupied. We had seen nobody in the halls as we entered the building, and many of the apartments were plainly empty.

"All the people in this building been questioned," the cop informed us, "and none of 'em, or the janitor, ever seen this dead guy before."

"We'll see the janitor ourselves," O'Malley decided.

* * * *

We had some trouble finding him. We knocked on several doors, at most of which we got no response, and finally located him in his living quarters in the basement. He was a huge, rather brutal-looking man, who plainly resented being questioned.

"How long since anybody lived in that place?" O'Malley asked him.

"T'ree mont'."

"Was it locked when the dead guy got in there?"

"Yah. Always lock'."

"Who had the keys?"

"I had him."

"Were the keys you had the only ones to the place?"

The janitor scowled at us. "I get back two key. That's right. Maybe somebody gets key made and I don't know. It's the same lock because nobody live there."

"What does he mean, O'Malley?" I inquired.

"I guess he means that when they rent an apartment they change the lock and give the tenant two keys. Sometimes tenants get extra keys made and he don't know about it. This is the same lock that was on the place when the last tenant occupied it, because it has been vacant. . . . How'd you come to go in there today when you found the dead guy?" he asked the janitor.

The janitor peered at us a long time silently. "I just go in," he answered finally.

"What was the name of the people who last lived there?"

"I think Andris."

As we were leaving, the janitor's wife came in. She was a coarsely pretty kid and she sparkled with costume jewelry. We went back upstairs to the entrance of the building.

"That janitor isn't telling all he knows, O'Malley," I declared. "He seems to be the only one who had access to that apartment and, according to his story, he just 'happened' to go in there and find the dead man. It doesn't sound right to me. He's married to a flirtatious woman about half his age, and that always causes trouble. The janitor's a lot smarter than he acts."

"Yeah; he's smart, all right. The guy had been dead three days. I don't think the dame had nothing to do with it, and I guess we won't get nothing out of the janitor. We'll call up headquarters and get them started looking for those Andris people."

"You think they may have kept a key?"

* * * *

We went to a drug store on the corner and O'Malley called up headquarters and came out of the booth smiling.

"They got the guy identified," he stated. "Every once in a while headquarters ain't so dumb. The chief thought, because his clothes was gone, he might be a rent collector; so they called up the building management companies and they learned a guy named Millen, that worked for a company called Lincoln & Wells, had been gone three days. So somebody from their office went down and recognized him."

"Explain why they thought that because of the clothes."

"Rent collectors is cagey guys, always looking to be held up; so they put money in their shoes and in their hats and sometimes they wear a money belt."

"Yes," I said, "and rent collectors go around in buildings and in that way meet a lot of women. I stick to the idea of the janitor's wife. You're wasting time, O'Malley, if you don't arrest the janitor."

"You got a lot of ideas. I wish some of 'em was good ones. We'll go see Lincoln & Wells."

We went to the office of the building management company and saw Mr. Wells.

"What did Millen go to that building for, Mr. Wells?" O'Malley asked him.

"That's inexplicable. That building is not under our management and he cannot have gone there on business. He was undoubtedly carrying several hundred dollars, and he was a careful man, and I cannot imagine his going into a building he knew nothing about."

"You tell us what his job was."

"Most of the tenants in buildings which we manage pay their rent by check or come here to the office and pay it. Every month there are a number who, for various reasons, are delinquent. Millen called on those people and collected the rent when possible and, if they could not pay, received their explanations."

"You know where he would have gone that day?"

"Approximately."

* * * *

Wells sent for a list and showed it to us. It gave the street numbers of something over half a dozen buildings and the names of several times that number of tenants. There were some folders on Wells' desk with a map of that part of New York, and O'Malley took one and marked the location of the buildings on it with a lead pencil.

We came out of the place.

"What's the idea?" I asked.

"A guy that's got a job like Millen had don't do any more traveling than is necessary. He might start at the building nearest the office and work away from it, or he might start farthest away and work back. Anyway, I figure he'd take 'em in some regular order. I'm going around to 'em and see if we can find out where he went that day."

We went to the building nearest to the office. It was on West End Avenue. Millen, it proved, had been there between nine and ten o'clock on the morning of the murder. All the tenants who were behind in their rent had seen him. At the second building, which was on Eightieth Street, and the third on Eighty-sixth, it was the same way. At the fourth building none of the tenants had seen Millen in several weeks.

"I begin to see through this," I commented. "After Millen left the building on Eighty-sixth Street he would naturally have come here. He never got here, so whatever happened to him began somewhere between."

"You try to make it easy. We're only guessing he'd have come here. We don't know where he went when he left that building."

"What were you expecting to find?" I asked.

"I thought maybe we'd find some building where some of them had seen Millen and some of 'em hadn't; then we'd know that what happened to him started in that building. Well, I'm going to quit and start again tomorrow."

I met him the next day.

"Headquarters dug up something that might interest you," he told me. "This Andris family that lived in that apartment went to South America when they left there."

"Then it doesn't matter whether they kept a key or not."

"It looks that way."

"So," I said triumphantly, "we come back to the janitor who was the only one who did have a key."

"I don't guess he had anything to do with it."

We took up where we had left off the night before and visited another building. The tenants had not seen Millen.

"We've got only one building left," O'Malley said. "It's on Amsterdam Avenue and there's only one guy there ain't paid his rent, and I can't fit it in how Millen would have went there."

"The Eighty-sixth Street building," I said, "is nearest the one where the body was found. You can take it from me that he went directly from Eighty-sixth Street, where we lost track of him, to where they found him."

"We'll finish the job, though, by going to this Amsterdam Avenue place."

We went out there. The one tenant who had not paid his rent was named Jaklin. A large-framed blond woman opened the door and her husband, who was a heavy-featured, unintelligent-looking man, sat by a window reading a newspaper. O'Malley made his usual inquiry.

"If you're from Lincoln & Wells," the man said, "I went to their office and paid my rent yesterday. Show 'em the receipt, Hilda."

The woman brought the receipt.

"That's all right," O'Malley told them. "I guess you promised Millen that you'd do that."

"We ain't seen Millen. He ain't been here for a month."

"Well, you won't see him again."

O'Malley sat down.

"No," the man agreed. "I saw that in yesterday's newspaper. Who knocked him off?"

"Nobody knows. But whoever done it picked up a nice piece of money."

"He had money on him, did he?"

"He'd collected several hundred dollars' rent, but that wasn't anything. This guy Millen didn't believe in banks."

The man and woman looked at each other. O'Malley got up to go.

"What do you mean, he didn't believe in banks?" the man inquired with interest.

"He'd lost some money in a bank once, so he didn't trust 'em. He kept his savings on him. He had about three thousand dollars in bills sewed up inside his clothes, and whoever done the murder must have knew that and took the clothes along."

We went out.

"Where did you get that information about money in Millen's clothes, O'Malley?" I asked curiously.

He looked at me with a queer expression. "I heard it this morning. Well, now we've been to all these places and got nothing. I'm going over to the precinct station and sit around."

"If that's all you're going to do," I said, "I'll leave you."

"I'd advise you to come along."

* * * *

We went to the precinct station and O'Malley went into the captain's room and talked with somebody while I waited outside. He came out again and sat down and we didn't do anything. At one o'clock I went and got some lunch, but O'Malley wouldn't go with me, and I brought him back a sandwich. Still we didn't do anything except talk with the desk officer when he wasn't answering the phone or talking with somebody else. About three o'clock the phone rang and the officer answered it.

"This is for you," he told O'Malley.

"Where from?"

"Queensboro Bridge."

We went out and got into a police car and drove over Queensboro Bridge. When we got near Flushing a plain-clothes cop who was sitting on the curbstone stopped us and got in with us and jerked his thumb toward a side street and we turned that way.

We were near Flushing Bay. There were coal yards and other business places. The tide was out and the wet mud was gleaming, and there were marshes and rank vegetation which hid small shacks. Then we came to a second plain-clothes cop sitting in some bushes. He got up and we followed him and came to a shack, and went around to the door and looked in, and there sat Jaklin pulling apart some muddy clothes. He started up and tried to get away from us but the cops grabbed him.

"All right, fellow," O'Malley told him. "You're the guy we want."

* * * *

"Clear this up for me, O'Malley," I said, somewhat later. "I saw what you did but I don't understand it."

"Why, when we found this Millen was a rent collector, I figured this wasn't nothing but a case of murder for robbery. Millen was a cautious guy and took no chances, so whatever happened to him happened while he was carrying on his business. But there hadn't nothing happened in the buildings we went to because the tenants all corroborated each other. They all said he was there and went away, or else that he hadn't come there. The one place something could have happened to him was at Jaklin's, because Jaklin didn't have no corroboration. Jaklin hadn't paid his rent and after Millen was dead he paid it, but we didn't have no evidence against him.

"I figured, when Millen came there to collect the rent, Jaklin might have made some excuse to get him to go to the other building with him, and then knocked him off. He took his clothes off to see if he had money hidden, and afterward he carried the clothes away with him to make it harder to identify him. He'd searched the clothes, of course; but when I told him and his wife Millen had money sewed into his clothes, they thought Jaklin must have overlooked it. I guess him and his wife had quite a pretty argument before Jaklin made up his mind to come out here and fish up the clothes again. They tell me he had business pretty often in Flushing and, after he'd killed Millen, he seems to have brought the clothes out and sunk 'em in Flushing Bay. Of course I'd had him watched."

"But," I said, still thinking of the janitor, "how did Jaklin get into the apartment? How about the key?"

"I don't know about the key."

When we got to the police station they had Mrs. Jaklin there and they took both their pedigrees. When they asked Mrs. Jaklin who her relatives were, she said she had none except a brother in South America.

"Your brother named Andris?" O'Malley asked her.

She saw she'd made a slip and wouldn't answer; finally she nodded.

"There's your key!" O'Malley whispered to me. "I guess when Millen come for the rent, Jaklin told him his brother-in-law had the money, and Millen went with him to get it. They probably knocked on the door and got no answer, and it didn't excite Millen's suspicions that Jaklin had a key to his brother-in-law's apartment."

"Good for you, O'Malley!" I commended. "This was nice work!"

"Yeah? There ain't nobody but you going to think that. They're going to think Jaklin was so dumb that anybody could have caught him."

THE HIGH BRIDGE

Originally published in *Collier's*, November 12, 1932.

"This is that case," said O'Malley, "that ain't never been solved yet, of the so-ciety guy that got killed in his apartment. It might be that you remember it. Re-nand his name was, and they thought his wife killed him but they could never get enough proof even to arrest her. These were pretty gay folks and they had an apartment in New York, and a house in Westchester and knew a lot of other gay guys and went to parties. Him and her had went to a party that night and gone home and he got shot."

"Certainly I remember it," I said. "There was stir enough about it. She said burglars did it. Some jewels were missing and were never found, but there was no other sign of burglars and nobody believed her. What's reopened that case?"

"Mrs. Renand herself got killed last night. She wouldn't go near the apart-ment after her husband got shot, and she lived in Westchester, but she come in town a lot. Last night she was driving herself homo from a party she had went to in Manhattan and her car went off the high bridge above the Speedway."

"What's that got to do with whether she killed her husband?"

"Not a thing; but us cops have to act wise. They want to know did she maybe leave something that would show she killed him. I won't find nothing because she was too smart a dame to leave evidence around."

* * * *

On the way out to Westchester we stopped to look at the spot where it had happened.

A section of the heavy iron railing of Washington Bridge was being repaired and had been replaced by planks, and the car had gone through the planks. Far below us we could see the treetops and the Harlem River and the Speedway, and we could see marks on the driveway where the car had landed, but the car had been taken away.

"It must be a terrible sensation," I said in a hushed voice, "to be in a car and feel it plunging from a height like this! O'Malley, do you think she did it on pur-pose?"

"How come?"

"She killed her husband and it has weighed on her ever since until it became too much for her. Last night, driving home alone, she saw the gap in the rail and drove her car through it."

"Yeah? If this lady felt bad because her husband got killed she never showed it, and if you think she was the kind that would knock herself off you ought to be locked up. Outside of them two things you might be right."

We went to the garage where they had taken the car. It had been a jewel-like piece of work but now all you could tell was that it once had been an automobile. I was interested in seeing what had happened to a car which had fallen from such a height. The motor had been shattered into fragments, but the gasoline tank was intact though battered, the horn would sound and the gear-shift still worked, as I ascertained by shifting it.

"Very interesting," I commented—"if it had anything to do with anything else."

"That's right. It would be. Anything been done to this bus since when it fell?" O'Malley asked the garage attendant.

"No, buddy; that's what I call a wreck. We picked her up with a crane and set her on a truck, and picked her off of the truck and set her there."

We got back into our car and drove to Westchester. The Renand house was not large, but was handsome and stood in carefully kept grounds. There was a middle-aged housekeeper and other servants. A car was parked in the driveway in the yard and a young man was talking with the housekeeper.

"This is a dreadful happening, gentlemen!" the young man said.

"It is that," O'Malley answered. "What's it got to do with you?"

"I was engaged to marry her."

"This is Mr. Innes," the housekeeper said.

"How long you been engaged to Mrs. Renand?" O'Malley asked.

"About a month."

"How long had you known her before that?"

"I've known her about six months."

"You didn't know her before Mr. Renand got shot?"

"No; I didn't meet her until some months afterward. I didn't know about this terrible accident until I saw it in the morning paper. Then I went where they had her and afterward I came out here."

"O. K., Mr. Innes," O'Malley told him.

We went into the house and the housekeeper went with us.

"What do you think of that guy?" O'Malley asked me. "He's a good-looking young guy but it don't make no difference to him if Mrs. Renand shot Renand or not—he wanted to marry her anyway. This Mrs. Renand was the kind of dame that sets 'em crazy, and I bet there's half a dozen other guys that felt the same about her. You'd think guys took pleasure being shot at."

"When a person once gets into trouble you police never let them alone," the housekeeper remarked.

"We got to do our business, lady."

The housekeeper made no objection when O'Malley told her he intended to search the house, but she went along to watch us doing it. In a pleasant room on the second floor, connecting with Mrs. Renand's bedroom, we found a desk whose pigeonholes were filled with letters.

"We might learn something now," O'Malley stated.

He seated himself at the desk and examined the letters. Occasionally he handed me one to look at. They wore nearly all letters from admiring men.

"This dame was a gay lady," O'Malley said, "and it looks like she got gayer after her husband died. Here's letters from this young Innes that we seen downstairs and it was like he said—he only met her a few months ago; and letters from a lot of other guys. Some of 'em sign their names but some sign only their initials. Here's, one guy wrote to her a lot but not lately, and he signs himself 'E.' Who would that be?" he asked the housekeeper.

She took the letter and examined it. "It might be Mr. Ewerson," she answered. "He used to be here quite a great deal."

"Yeah? Who's he?"

"You can see his house from the drive in front of this one."

Presently O'Malley bundled the letters back into their pigeonholes. "Nothing in those," he said.

There was nothing else of importance in the desk, If Mrs. Renand had left a confession she had left it somewhere else.

We searched the whole house thoroughly. In a disused bureau under discarded clothes we found a small package wrapped in chamois skin and, as O'Malley unwrapped it, I saw diamonds glistening. There were several rings set with large stones and a brooch set with many smaller ones.

"I don't remember the description of the jewels which Mrs. Renand said were stolon when her husband was killed," I remarked, "but I shall be much surprised if these are not the ones."

"These are the ones, all right."

"Then Mrs. Renand lied and the case is solved. She killed her husband. She hid the jewels, pretending that a burglar had taken them, and the police failed to find them. Since then, she could not bring herself to destroy them and there was no other way she could dispose of them for fear of their being traced to her."

"I guess you got the answer," O'Malley assented.

"So they weren't so crazy when they sent you out here!" I observed sarcastically.

"No; they was wise guys."

* * * *

The next morning I read in my newspaper that the Renand case finally had been solved, and I saw with pleasure that O'Malley's name was mentioned.

I didn't see O'Malley for a couple of days.

"What are you working on now?" I asked him when I met him.

"Same case."

I was astonished.

"I got interested," he explained, "in them guys that wrote her all those letters. I guess I'm a dumb cop to be going around asking questions after the case is solved. I seen most of the guys that wrote her, and I talked with all the people that was at the party that night when she started home alone."

"Learn anything?" I asked.

"Not a thing. I ain't seen that Ewerson yet, who signed his letters 'E'."

"Was Ewerson at the party?"

"No."

We went out to Ewerson's. He was a handsome man of forty with a tired face and weary eyes, and he received us politely but indifferently.

"I got some letters here I want to read you, Mr. Ewerson," O'Malley told him.

He took from his pocket a packet of letters which I recognized as those which had been in Mrs. Renand's desk, and read one and then another of them aloud. They seemed to me the sort of letters any man might write to a woman for whom he has an ardent admiration.

"You write those?"

Ewerson took the letters and examined them. "Yes; those are my letters."

"You wasn't home the night Mrs. Renand got killed, was you?"

"No. I was in New York and spent the night at a hotel. You'll find my name on the hotel register."

"Yeah, I found it. Did you see Mrs. Renand that night?"

Ewerson did not answer.

"You was at the hotel, all right," said O'Malley, "but I got evidence of a doorman, an elevator operator and a newsdealer that you left the hotel about half past one A. M. and didn't come back until about two hours later. That was the time when Mrs. Renand had her accident. Now I got something else I want to read to you."

O'Malley drew from among the letters a gray monogrammed envelope, opened it, and took out a sheet of note paper. I recognized envelope and paper as being like some I had seen in Mrs. Renand's desk marked with her initials.

"'If I should meet sudden death,'" he read, "'you may be certain that the one to be accused is Albert Ewerson. I will not explain why he should desire my death, but my protection is to have this in writing. I shall tell him I have written it!'"

I have never seen a man look more utterly weary than Ewerson. He seemed to consider something and come to a decision.

"She never told me she had written that," he said. "It was—rather like her. It is true, of course. I killed her."

He looked like a man putting down a burden which he had carried until it had become intolerable.

"You kill Renand, too?"

"Yes—by accident. Mrs. Renand and I had been—rather more than friends, and on the night of his death at the party which we all attended, Renand became suspicious of us. He demanded that I come to his apartment after the party. He was a jealous, violent man and before going to his apartment I obtained a revolver, but I had no idea of attacking him—it was purely for self-defense. I dreaded scandal and on reaching the apartment I avoided the elevator and walked up. Renand accused us and we admitted it. I was anxious to marry Mrs. Renand if she would leave him, but he grew wild with rage when I suggested that. He threatened me and I drew the revolver to protect myself, and in the struggle for it he was shot. Mrs. Renand fully realized that it had been an accident but we knew that no one else would believe that. No one knew that I had come there. She told me to go away before she gave the alarm and she would try to make it look as though it had been done by a burglar.

"We continued to see each other after that, but we did not dare to marry for fear it would bring up again the question of how Renand had died. Then some months ago Mrs. Renand met young Innes and became infatuated with him. I was losing her. Nothing in the world mattered to me except her, and I could not endure the thought of her belonging to someone else. I begged her for one more interview and, on the night of her death, she agreed that, after leaving the party, she would pick me up and drive me out here."

* * * *

O'Malley went to the telephone to call headquarters. As he did so, I took from his hand the paper containing Mrs. Renand's statement, opened it and looked at it. As I expected, there was no writing whatever on the sheet of notepaper.

47

"I see through most of this, O'Malley," I said, an hour later, "but not all of it. It's plain, of course, that you found reason to suspect Ewerson and used the old trick on him of reading an accusation against him which you pretended Mrs. Renand had left. I am surprised, however, that he fell for it."

"I ain't sure he did fall for it, but it wasn't necessary. He seen that we suspected him and would get him sooner or later, and besides, the guy loved this Mrs. Renand and he'd killed her and he doesn't care what happens to him."

"Was it his letters that made you suspect him?"

"There wasn't nothing in the letters. Hut the guy lived close to Mrs. Renand and still he was always writing to her, and when she got engaged to this Innes his letters stopped. I asked about where he had been that night, and he couldn't be accounted for at the time she got killed."

"But how did he do it?"

"I figure he done it this way: He'd noticed where the bridge rail was being fixed and that gave him the idea. He knew she was going to the party that night and he got her to pick him up afterward because that late there wouldn't be much traffic on the bridge. She didn't have no idea he meant to harm her. He begged her to break her engagement to this Innes and she wouldn't. When they got near the bridge he made an excuse to get her to stop the car, and knocked her unconscious and run the car off the bridge so it would look like an accident."

"Yes; and he almost got away with it. By everybody except you it was accepted as an accident. That's the part of it that I don't understand."

"You seen Mrs. Renand's car."

"I did," I said indignantly, "and there was nothing about that piece of wreckage which could tell you anything."

"You're always making me think you ain't very bright. The car was in low gear. You tried the gears yourself and they couldn't have been jarred from high speed into low. Would any lady run her car off of a bridge in low by accident? It had to be murder or suicide, and this wasn't no lady that would kill herself. I figured somebody had started the car and then stepped out of it and watched it go off the bridge."

"That was police work, O'Malley!" I said approvingly, "and you'll get credit for it because the newspapers have already mentioned you in the case."

"Sure they mentioned me," he said, "when we had it solved wrong, but you'll see they won't say nothing about me now that we got it solved right."

TOO MANY ENEMIES

Originally published in *Collier's*, February 11, 1933.

"This is one of them vengeance murders," said O'Malley, "and in this kind of case plenty people know who done it but they all go blind and dumb. I'll have no luck with it. This dead guy was named Vanelli, and he was only twenty-three years old but already he had so many enemies it was only a question who would get him first. They got plenty cops working on this case."

"How was he killed?" I asked.

"He got beat up and then stabbed."

"Where?"

"Right in his own home. This Vanelli got himself suspected of passing info to the cops about some guys he knew that done a little counterfeiting; and, besides that, a guy that he had went with for a long time but had had trouble with got knocked off and the guy's family thought Vanelli had a hand in it; and when he already had two outfits trying to shove him over, Vanelli goes to Boston and runs off with a girl that was going to marry somebody else."

"He sounds like a desperate character," I said.

"The guy got himself so he couldn't be nothing but desperate. We'll go and look at him."

We went. Vanelli seemed to have been an ordinary-looking young man, but it was not easy to tell much about that now. As O'Malley had said, he had been badly beaten up. His nose was broken and his face battered and he had been stabbed five times and the letter Z had been cut on both his cheeks.

"What was the name of the man whose girl he ran away with?" I inquired.

"Zeglio."

"Well!" I exclaimed triumphantly. "What more do you want?"

"You're smart."

They had Vanelli's clothes there and we examined them carefully. He had been stabbed twice in the back and three times in front, but his clothes were stabbed twice in front and three times in back.

"I suppose," I hazarded, "that after the first stabbing there was a struggle and his clothes got twisted around his body so that the holes don't correspond."

"You can account for everything, can't you!" O'Malley commented. "We'll see what Zeglio says about it."

They had already arrested Zeglio and had him at the station house, so we went there. The station house looked as though they were holding a convention. Vanelli's parents were there and had identified the body and now wanted to claim it. Besides Zeglio, they had the girl there, and several members of the family who believed that Vanelli had put their relative on the spot, and a number of the men who were suspected of counterfeiting. They all talked at once and I had never seen such excitable people, and most of them seemed to be congratulating one another that Vanelli was dead.

They had Zeglio and the girl kept separate and we talked with her first. She was a beautiful girl, about seventeen years old, with hair black as night and dark limpid eyes, and she couldn't make the simplest statement without putting emotion into it. Her name was Josephina.

"For why am I kept here?" she demanded passionately before we had a chance to question her.

"They got to have you for a witness, lady."

"But I know nothing. I have told all. For how long will I be kept?"

"It might be quite a while, girlie. You tell us over again what it was you told them."

"I told nothing because I know nothing. I was making dinner and wondering when Peter would come home." Peter was Vanelli. "Then I heard something— like quarreling. Two people. I look out but see no one. Then I heard something like fighting, but I can see nobody. Again a third time I look out, wondering when Peter will come, and Peter is in front of the door."

"Was he dead?" O'Malley asked.

"Certainly he was dead."

"Was one of the voices you heard Peter's?"

"If I had thought that I would have gone to look."

"Was one of them Zeglio's?"

"I don't know. Now I have told everything, so why do you keep me here?"

I was sorry for her.

"That's a wonderful girl, O'Malley," I said, after we had left her, "and I don't wonder there was trouble over her; it's a shame to keep her locked up."

"Yeah, I saw you thought she was a knock-out. You keep on thinking that and you might get a knife pushed into you yourself."

We questioned Zeglio. He was a small man, dark, quick and muscular.

"You knock Vanelli off?" O'Malley asked him.

"Not me." Zeglio grinned at us delightedly.

"How long ago did you come from Boston?"

"This time, ten days."

"You'd been here before, then. When was that?"

"Two months."

"I see. That was when Vanelli run off with your girl. You came here and looked for them, intending to kill him, but you couldn't find them. So you went back and ten days ago you came again."

"Thata right, I keela heem if I geta the chance."

"And last night you got the chance and stuck a knife in him and left him outside of Josephina's door."

"Not me. Some other guy. I looka ten days but I don't find heem."

"And this other guy cut your initials in his cheeks?"

Zeglio shrugged. "What a kind guy," he answered. "He beata me to it."

We talked with the other people there and they all made the same answer as Zeglio. They admitted that they had intended to kill Vanelli and had been looking for him, but he and the girl had hidden themselves and they had been unable to find him. Now someone else, they said, had killed him, but they didn't know who. We went to look at the place where it had happened.

It was a rather nice apartment building on the West Side. Vanelli and the girl had had an apartment in the rear. A long hall led through the building and a shorter hall branched off to the door of Vanelli's apartment. There was blood on the floor of the long hall and more blood in front of Vanelli's door, and a uniformed cop was on post in the hall and another one in the apartment.

We looked everything over carefully. There were two rooms with a bathroom between them, and someone had spilled a bottle of ink on the floor in front of the bathroom door. Otherwise the place was spotlessly clean. Vanelli's clothes and the girl's clothes were hanging in closets, and there was a table set with two places, and the dinner Josephina had been cooking was still on the stove. Some of Josephina's things had been put into a suitcase. I thought she had been getting them ready to take with her to the police station, and I was indignant that they had hurried her away without them.

"What do you make of it, O'Malley?" I asked.

"I don't make nothing of it. This case is like I said; everybody we talked to has been lying, and you can't solve a case where nobody tells the truth."

"At least one of them is lying," I agreed, "because one of them killed Vanelli. But the others, in that case, would be telling the truth, and I am quite sure that Josephina told it."

"Yeah? How do you figure that?"

"The quarreling she heard was in the long hall where she couldn't see the speakers. Vanelli was killed there. Afterward the murderer carried or dragged him into the short hall and put him in front of the door, and when Josephina looked out she found him."

"You make it sound pretty good."

I was pleased at his commendation, so I went on: "I have come to the conclusion, O'Malley, that it was done by Zeglio."

"All right; let's hear it."

"At first I thought the Z's on Vanelli's cheeks meant that someone was trying to throw suspicion on Zeglio and meant he really hadn't done it; but this was a murder of revenge. A man seeking revenge is willing to take a risk if there is someone whom he wants to have know he did it. Zeglio wanted Josephina to know. What, do you think of that?"

"I guess it deserves consideration. . . . Who spilled the ink on the floor?" O'Malley asked the officer.

"Search *me*," the officer replied. "It was that way when we come here."

O'Malley scraped up some of the ink and put it in an envelope.

"Anything been taken away from here?" he asked the officer.

"Not a thing except the dead guy. We was told to keep it like it was."

"What are you looking for?" I asked O'Malley.

"People like this Vanelli and Josephina always have pictures of their folks around, and the first thing a guy like him does if he runs away with a girl is get his picture taken with her. Well, where's the pictures?"

I myself was surprised a little, now that he spoke of it. There was not a picture in the apartment. There were several photographers in the neighborhood, and after we came out of the apartment we went around to them and O'Malley asked them if any of them had taken a picture of Vanelli and Josephina. None of them had. As we were leaving the last place he noticed several different-sized small pictures of a darkhaired girl and asked the photographer about them.

"You sell any of these?" he questioned.

The photographer said he could not sell them, until O'Malley showed him his badge; then he agreed, and O'Malley picked out two of different sizes and we took them back to the apartment and gave them to the cop in the hall, but I couldn't hear what O'Malley said to him.

"What's that for?" I asked.

"There wasn't no pictures in the place, so I told the cop to put some there."

"That sounds like a silly performance to me."

"That's right; it might turn out to be silly."

"What I like least in this case," I said, "is your keeping Josephina locked up."

"You'll get that knife in you yet if you keep on thinking about her."

"She hasn't done anything," I said, "and it is clear now that she told the truth. I admit that she eloped with Vanelli and was living with him without being married to him, but that was to get away from Zeglio. She and Vanelli undoubtedly meant to get married, and I don't blame her for what she did under the circumstances. But now you have her locked up, and the way you are going about it there seems no chance of Vanelli's murder being solved, so there is no telling how long she'll have to stay there, or what people are going to think about her. You're putting a stigma on the girl which she doesn't deserve."

"I was thinking maybe we'd ought to let her go."

"If you're afraid of losing track of her you can have her watched."

We went back to the police station and O'Malley went into the captain's office but I stayed outside. I knew he was arranging to have Josephina released, and I would have been glad to have her know that I had had a hand in it, but I didn't get the chance to tell her.

When he came out we went back to the apartment, hut we didn't go in. Instead we went into a shoe-repair place across the street. The proprietor asked what we wanted done to our shoes, but O'Malley told him "nothing," and we just sat and waited.

"Are you having her watched?" I asked.

"I guess we know where she'll go."

Presently I saw Josephina come along the street and go into the building opposite, and a plainclothesman who had been following her came in and sat down with us.

"Will the cops in there interfere with her?" I asked.

"There ain't no cops in there. I had 'em taken off."

* * * *

In about an hour Josephina came out of the building very hurriedly. She had her suitcase with her and she seemed much excited. She got into a cab, and after she had driven away we got into another cab and followed her. She went to the Bronx. The cab stopped in front of a rooming-house and the cabman carried in her bag for her, and after he had gone away we went in after her.

We could hear Josephina in one of the rooms talking loudly, and we listened for a moment. Then O'Malley and the other plainclothesman kicked down the door, and a handsome, reckless-looking young man to whom Josephina had been speaking violently jumped up at sight of us. Pieces of the photographs which O'Malley had bought were scattered on the floor.

"Okay, Vanelli," O'Malley said to the young man. "We want you for murder."

"This is all a mystery to me, O'Malley," I said about an hour later. "I can't see through it."

"What can't you see?" he asked. "This Vanelli was on the spot and he knew it. Him and the girl hid out, but he had too many people after him, and he knew wherever he went one of 'em would find him, and they were getting closer to him all the time. He figured if they thought he was dead they'd quit looking. We don't know yet who the dead guy was and we might never find out. There's plenty guys right now around the streets that got no jobs and their folks don't know where they are, and there's nobody to ask questions if one of 'em disappears. I guess Vanelli picked out one of 'em that looked something like himself and made some excuse to get him to go home with him—it might be he offered him a meal. When they got to the apartment Vanelli knocked him off. Then him and Josephina dressed the guy in Vanelli's clothes and Vanelli lit out, taking the guy's clothes with him, and Josephina give the alarm."

"So Josephina was in it with him?" I asked, depressed.

"I wouldn't wonder if Vanelli planned it all himself and she didn't know nothing about it till it had been done; but then she backed him up the same as his parents did. Vanelli's parents seen it wasn't their son, but they identified him anyway so that Vanelli could get away, and whatever other people saw him didn't know him very well and didn't question it being him because his parents said so. I told you this was a case where you had to figure that everybody was lying. I figure the murder happened inside the apartment in front of the bathroom door. Vanelli stabbed the guy and pushed him into the bathroom where it was all tile and the blood could be washed up. I guess they undressed and dressed him in the bathtub. Some blood got on the floor outside the bathroom door where he was stabbed, and it couldn't be washed up clean and so they poured ink on it. I got some of the ink off the floor being analyzed now to see if they find blood in it and I'm sure they will."

"But," I said, "you seem to have realized from the first that the dead man wasn't Vanelli. How was that?"

"Why, the guy was wearing his own clothes when he got stabbed, and then they dressed him in Vanelli's clothes and they had to poke holes in them; but it was a hard job to get the holes exactly where the wounds was, and they didn't get it right. If he wasn't wearing Vanelli's clothes when he got killed, he wasn't Vanelli. They put blood off the guy's clothes in two places in the hall to make it look as if the murder happened outside the apartment, and Vanelli cut the Z's in the guy's cheeks so we'd think it was done by Zeglio.

"I guess Vanelli and the girl had it planned to meet later in some other city and start over where they wasn't known. She was altogether too anxious to get released by the police so she could join him; but we couldn't let her go for fear she'd disappear. Then I and you went to the apartment. They had to leave Vanelli's clothes there so as not to excite suspicions, and her things were there too. If she was released, she'd have to go there to get her things and when she did that she'd go through Vanelli's clothes to be sure there wasn't nothing being left in 'em.

"I didn't know whether she knew where Vanelli was or not; but I figured she was the kind of girl that, if she found some other girl's picture in Vanelli's clothes, would forget about everything else until she had found out about it. So I got a couple of pictures of another girl and had one of the cops put 'em in

Vanelli's pockets. She found 'em, all right; and she went straight to Vanelli to get an explanation about 'em."

"It was a remarkable case," I said, "and I'm surprised that you got the answer to it so quickly."

"Sure. It's a swell case, but too many other cops was working on it. You watch and see who they say figured this all out. It won't be me."

NO FINGERPRINTS

Originally published in *Collier's*, March 18, 1933.

"The case I got now," O'Malley said, "a girl got murdered. This was in Greenwich Village. She went and took a couple of rooms and told the landlady she was going to get married and her husband would come and live with her. The next time the landlady seen her she'd been knocked off."

"Is that all they know about it?" I inquired.

"She give her name as Miss Neal and told where she worked. That's all they know. We'll go and look at her."

We did. She was pretty and about twenty-two years old and had a small, determined face. She'd been hit in the head.

"They got anything about this lady yet?" O'Malley asked the attendant.

"I guess they have. Two cops was here with a young guy. He looked at her and then he said, 'It's her,' and then they all went over to the station-house."

"Well," said O'Malley, "I guess we got to find out what we can about it."

We went to the precinct station. The young man was twenty-four or -five years old and he looked pale and horrified and shaken. It appeared his name was Robert Elwood.

"This young fellow," one of the officers told us, "come here a couple of days ago and said the girl he was engaged to, named Miss Neal, had disappeared, and he wanted us to look for her. He had a note from her saying she was going to marry someone else, so the captain told him to go on home, it wasn't police business. When we got this homicide, we went and told him. It's his girl, all right."

"You tell us about this," O'Malley directed Elwood.

"Mary never told me that she didn't mean to marry me," Elwood said unsteadily. "Then I got that note from her. I couldn't understand what had happened. I went to where she worked, and they said she hadn't quit her job but just hadn't come back to it. Then I went to where she'd lived, but she'd moved and hadn't left any address. So then I came to the police but they wouldn't do anything. Mary was alone in New York and you police were supposed to protect her. Well, you didn't do it! Why don't you get busy and get the man who did this, instead of standing around here asking questions?"

"I don't guess you kept that note?" O'Malley asked him.

"Of course I did."

Elwood held out the note. O'Malley looked at it and then put it in his pocket.

"You ever see this guy she writes about?"

"I think once I did. I didn't know he meant anything to her. It was just I saw a man talking with her and then he walked away. I didn't see him very well. He was tall and had a small mustache."

"It might be you could identify him, then. How'd it come this note is typewritten?"

"She typewrote all her letters. She was a stenographer."

"You got any of them letters?"

"Plenty."

"You might bring 'em in and leave 'em with the desk officer."

"Let's see that note, O'Malley," I said after we had left the station.

It didn't help any. It said, "I hate to hurt you but I can't help it because I love someone else. I'm going to marry him. Please don't ever look for me."

"Not much in that," I commented.

"Not anything. We'll see the landlady."

We went. It was a five-story "walk-up" building of furnished apartments. First we looked at it from outside; then we went in. The landlady lived in the basement.

"This girl," she told us, "came here and wanted an apartment. She gave the firm she worked for as a reference. I had two vacant, one on the fourth floor, one on the fifth. She looked at both of them and took the fifth and paid me a deposit. That same night she moved in, with a trunk and couple of suitcases, but after that I didn't see her. After a couple of days I got curious and looked in with a pass-key. Well, she was there—the same way the police found her later!"

"She say anything about this guy she intended to marry?"

"Only mentioned him. She said she was a lot in love with him and it might cause trouble."

"Anybody come here to see her?"

"Not a soul."

"Who else you show those apartments to these last few days?"

"Not anyone."

"Let's see 'em."

We followed her upstairs and looked at the fourth-floor apartment and then went to the fifth, which was directly over it. A uniformed cop was asleep there in an easy-chair. We woke him up and he told us not to touch anything because the fingerprint men hadn't been there yet. There were two rooms, exactly like the two rooms on the floor below, arranged the same and with the same kind of fire-place, and there were a shovel and a pair of tongs there, but there was no poker.

"The homicide guys took the poker away with 'em," the cop remarked to us. "She was killed with that—I guess you know. They didn't find no prints on it, they tell me."

"They find any pictures of men among her things?"

"Not any."

"You'd think she'd have a picture of the guy she was going to marry."

"He'd be a dumb guy if he didn't carry that away with him."

We looked the place over carefully without touching things where it would leave a print, but we didn't find anything. Then we went back downstairs.

"She must have liked to walk upstairs," I commented. "The fourth-floor apartment is exactly like the one on the fifth, but she took the top one."

"No," O'Malley said, "they're different. The top one has got a vacant apartment underneath it."

"Are you suggesting," I inquired with sarcasm, "that this young woman carefully selected a place with a vacant apartment underneath, so that she could be safely murdered without anyone's hearing?"

"I think somebody did. She had been dead two days, according to the medical guys."

We went to the place where she had worked and afterward to the boarding-house where she had lived and we talked with everybody at both places. Elwood had seen all of them when he was trying to find her, but none of them had ever met the man with the small mustache. Some of them thought they'd seen him.

"The way of a maid, O'Malley!" I observed. "All these people know about the man she didn't intend to marry, but the one she meant to marry she never introduced to any of them."

"That's right. How do you figure it?"

"He may be a married man," I said importantly.

"You're pretty smart. Well, we done a lot of work and got nothing by it, and I'm ready to call it a day and start again tomorrow morning—and I guess we won't get nothing then, either."

I met him the next morning.

"Elwood's taking them letters to the precinct station-house," he stated. "I said we'd meet him there."

We went to the station-house and found Elwood there. He had a half-dozen letters and O'Malley looked them over carefully, but there was nothing in them of importance.

"Nothing in these," O'Malley said. "This is one case where we ain't got a single lead, unless it might be we missed something at that apartment. I'm going there again. Will you come with us?" he invited Elwood.

"If I can be of help. You don't seem to be getting anywhere. Why don't you get that man?"

We went to the apartment.

"This place been fingerprinted yet?" O'Malley asked the cop on duty there.

"Not yet."

"What's the matter with them guys? You two got gloves. Better put 'em on."

Elwood and I put on our gloves.

"I been tryin' to think out how this job was done," O'Malley said gloomily. "I figure the guy come here the same night the girl moved in. She hadn't got unpacked yet. He took care no one seen him come in. Then what? When her hack was turned he hit her with the poker. Well, where was he before that? I figure while he was planning how he'd do it, he stepped in the kitchen. When she was busy and her back was turned, he stepped out again. That brought him to the poker. He picked that up and had to make one more step."

He put out his hand to take hold of the edge of the kitchen door and show us what he meant; then he remembered about fingerprints and didn't touch it.

"I want this place printed," he declared.

He said something to the cop and then he and I went downstairs and telephoned the identification bureau. They said they'd send a fingerprint man immediately. When we got back upstairs the cop was standing in the fifth-floor hall and Elwood was looking out the window of the apartment. The fingerprint man got there in about twenty minutes and blew his powders on all the smooth surfaces in the place.

"No prints except the girl's," he said.

"You try that kitchen door."

He tried it. "No prints at all here."

"The guy was too smart for us," O'Malley said in discouragement.

We went back to the street and parted with Elwood. When we got around the corner O'Malley started to run, until we found a cab.

"We got to move quick!"

He gave the cabman an address but I didn't know where we were going until we got to the East Side place where Elwood lived.

"Mr. Elwood said he'd meet us here," O'Malley told the landlady.

"His door must be unlocked, then. Third floor, the room in front."

We went up. The door was locked but O'Malley found a way to open it. He searched the place as fast as he could. In the space under a dresser drawer he found a dozen letters and six of them were the same as the ones that Elwood had given us, but they were written with a different typewriter.

"What's the meaning of this?" I demanded in bewilderment.

O'Malley didn't answer me because there was an interruption. Elwood had come in the door.

"What's the idea?" he shouted.

O'Malley got between him and the door. "No idea at all, except I'm going to put the cuffs on you for murder, Robert."

Elwood was quick. He was halfway out the window when we caught him by the legs.

"What *is* all this, O'Malley?" I demanded, after we had taken Elwood to the station-house.

"This Elwood's people live in Washington. We got a wire on him now at headquarters from the Washington police. There's a girl there with plenty of dough his folks want him to marry, but he'd got mixed up with this Mary Neal they didn't know about, and she wasn't the kind he could break off with without her making trouble. So he schemed to get rid of her. I figure he picked that apartment without ever going in it, because he could see it had a vacant one underneath it, and he told her to take it so they could live in it when they was married. Then he went there and knocked her off. He knew he'd be the first one questioned when they found her, so he beat us to it by coming to the station-house and saying she had disappeared. There wasn't no guy with a small mustache."

"Of course," I said, "he wrote that farewell letter to himself."

"You're getting good. When I asked him for her other letters he seen that if they weren't on the same machine he'd be suspected. So he had to copy them. There ain't any typewriter in his place, so I guess we'll find he used one at the place he works. He's a smart guy, but smart guys have dumb spots in 'em. It was a dumb spot when he kept the letters after copying 'em."

"But," I objected, "I'm sure when we went to that apartment this morning, you only suspected him, and when we came away you knew that he was guilty. How was that?"

"You forget the kitchen door."

"There were no marks on the kitchen door," I said indignantly.

"There'd ought to have been. I put mine on when you two wasn't looking."

I didn't get it. Then suddenly I did.

"Good Lord!" I exclaimed. "You put your fingerprints on the edge of the door without his knowing it. Then you and I went to telephone and you'd told the cop to step out into the hall. Elwood had been careful not to leave fingerprints when he did the murder, but he couldn't remember whether he'd touched the kitchen door or not, and he took the chance to wipe it off. When the fingerprint expert found no prints there, you knew Elwood was guilty. You're one clever cop, O'Malley!"

"I wish you was police commissioner, then I might get promoted. So far, the only guy I can make think I'm smart is you."

TOO MANY MILES

Originally published in *Collier's*, April 1, 1933.

"This case," said O'Malley, "a truck owner got knocked over. This fellow had a fleet of trucks and rented 'em, and sometimes I guess he rented some to rum-runners. Well, he was on Long Island for some reason. Then they found his car and looked up the license—Mawson his name was. Then they found him. He was in Jamaica Bay."

"What had been done to him?" I asked.

"He had been shot. A guy's got no chance to solve this kind of case, because he asks questions but nobody tells him the answers."

We started asking questions. We were at police headquarters. They had a hard-eyed, well-dressed young man there, named Kizer, and O'Malley began with him.

"You a bootlegger?" he inquired. "Speak up; I'm no enforcement officer."

"That's what I am."

"You rent some trucks from this dead guy the night that he got killed?"

"Not me. Some other fellows did. They delivered my part of the stuff to me all right. I don't know their names."

"In this case I guess nobody don't know any names."

Mrs. Mawson had been brought to headquarters, but had collapsed. A police surgeon had been taking care of her, and her own doctor had come there too. The doctors let us see her only a few minutes.

"What was your husband doing on Long Island that night?" O'Malley asked her.

"I have no idea. He never told me anything about his business."

"Did he know he was on the spot?"

"If he did, he kept it from me. He knew I was always afraid something like this might happen. He was always driving around alone at night."

"When did you see him last?"

"At dinner. The car was parked outside. After dinner he said he was going out and might be late, but I didn't think anything of that because it happened so often."

* * * *

Mrs. Mawson's doctor came out of the room with us. He was young and pleasant-spoken and his name was Landol.

"Mrs. Mawson is in no condition to remember details right now," he told us. "If she recalls anything that will be of help to you I'll make a note of it."

We thanked him.

"We'll go see where they found the guy," O'Malley decided.

We drove out to Jamaica Bay. There were marshes and innumerable inlets of the sea, and scores of small boats, some of which I did not doubt were rum-runners; and there were tire tracks in the marsh near where Mawson had been found, and O'Malley made careful note of them. We went then to look at Mawson. He didn't look as I expected a truck owner would look. He was a dapper little man about thirty-five years old, partly bald, and he had worn hornrimmed spectacles. His spectacles were broken. He had been tightly tied with several pieces of new rope, and the police had cut the rope.

"Are those seaman's knots, O'Malley," I inquired, "or were they tied by bootleggers?"

He looked at them. "Them knots don't mean a thing to me. We'll see his car."

We went to the garage where they had taken it. A Queensborough officer was in charge of it. It was a handsome car, and its tires were like the tire tracks in the marsh. There was no blood on it.

We examined it carefully and even took the cushions out of it to see if we could find pieces of the broken eyeglasses, but we couldn't find any.

"He wasn't killed in the car," O'Malley decided.

There was a piece of cardboard on the dash which said: "April 10. Mileage at last greasing of 9651."

O'Malley looked at the speedometer. "This guy had drove forty-seven miles since his car was greased," he commented.

"What of it?"

"Not anything, I guess."

"You Manhattan lads are a little late," the Queensborough cop informed us. "We already found out where this fellow got pushed over and we got the guy that done it."

That was news to us. He told us where to go and we went over there. It was a hot-dog and oyster lunchroom, with some rooms behind it, and the police had found blood on the floor of one of the rooms and some new rope like the pieces of rope Mawson had been tied with. The place was full of officers. They had arrested the proprietor. He was a heavy-set, plump-faced man named D'Angelino, and he had a young and darkly pretty wife.

"How about this, wop?" O'Malley asked him.

D'Angelino became excited; he gesticulated. "Two guys fight in da back room and make-a da nose bleed. Dees rope clothes-a-line da same like everybody have."

"You know a guy named Kizer?"

"Never meet-a da guy."

We went back to Manhattan.

"That was a short murder case," I commented.

"You think D'Angelino done it?"

"No; but I think he knows who did."

"You might be right, at that. How far we come from where Mawson's car was ditched till now?"

I hadn't noticed.

"We come sixteen miles," O'Malley informed me. "This Mawson had his car greased the day that he got killed, and he had went forty-seven miles afterward, and thirty-one of them miles we don't know where he went. But we don't know what time of day the greasing was done."

"Would it do any good to know that?"

"I guess not. I'd just like to know it."

We went to several garages near where Mawson had lived, and at the fourth one we found the mechanic who had greased the car.

"What time was that, buddy?" O'Malley asked him.

"Just before dinner, brother."

"Did he say anything else about it?"

"Sure. He said grease the car and take it to his house and leave it. I done that."

"Say anything more?"

"Sure. Said check the car all over and see that it was right because he was taking a long drive."

"Did he say where he was going?"

"Sure. Said he was going to Boston."

"It's a strange thing," I observed, "if he was going to Boston, that he didn't tell his wife."

"She was upset and it might be she forgot about it. Well, there's no use working on this case, because them smart Queensborough officers have beat us to it. So I guess I'll take in a picture show."

We separated.

"This Mawson," he said, the next time I met him, "drove plenty places looking after his trucks. He drove to New Jersey and to Philadelphia and sometimes to Boston. This time he drove out on Long Island and he never come back. But he drove too many miles."

"You don't know where he went before he got killed."

"You're getting smarter than you used to be, but I'd like to know where he done all that mileage."

We drove out on Long Island to where Mawson's car was found.

"Notice how far we go," O'Malley directed as we started on again.

We went north across the island. At College Point we took the ferry to The Bronx. From there we drove into Westchester and made a circuit and came back to Manhattan, but we didn't stop anywhere till we got where Mawson lived.

"How far?" O'Malley asked.

"It happens," I replied sarcastically, "that we have traveled just about forty-seven miles, but if that has anything to do with this case I'm a Dutchman."

"Yeah? We'll ask Mrs. Mawson."

But we didn't ask Mrs. Mawson. There was a nurse there who said the doctor had left orders that no one was to see Mrs. Mawson without his permission. The doctor would be there that evening.

We called up Doctor Landol's office, but he wasn't in; and then O'Malley called headquarters, but I didn't hear what he said to them.

"I didn't see no picture yesterday," he said, "because I thought of something else to do. We might see one now because we got plenty time."

We saw a picture. Afterward we went to headquarters but we merely loafed around. Then a uniformed cop and a plain-clothes man from Westchester came in with some new rope and some small pieces of glass sealed in an envelope.

"The guy's oculist," the plain-clothes man said, "says this glass is the same prescription that he gave him."

We went back to the Mawsons' but Dr. Landol told us Mrs. Mawson was too nervous to see anybody. O'Malley didn't seem to mind.

"You're a smart guy, Doc," he told the doctor, "but I guess we got to take you to the station-house for murder."

Landol tried to close the door on us but O'Malley had his foot in it. The doctor didn't say anything after we had forced our way in; he just went and got his hat and coat.

"Does Landol live in Westchester, O'Malley?" I asked a half hour later.

"You got it."

"But what had the bootleggers to do with it?"

"Are you that dumb? Not anything, and that guy D'Angelino didn't neither. This Dr. Landol and Mrs. Mawson was what they call 'too friendly.' She is young and kind of gay and the doc is a young guy too, and Mawson was out of town a lot. It seems Mawson found out about 'em. He had to go to Boston and he thought Landol would go to his wife, so he stopped to settle things with Landol and they had trouble to the point where Landol shot him.

"Mawson had plenty shady people renting his trucks that might have knocked him off, and Landol figured to make it look like it was one of them that done it, so as to keep himself and Mrs. Mawson out of it. He done Mawson up with rope like gangsters might have, and he put him in Mawson's car and took him to Long Island, and he pushed him out in Jamaica Bay and then he ditched the car. Afterward he come to town and told Mrs. Mawson. I guess they thought it would be safer if she didn't tell Mawson was going to Boston, because to get to Boston he would have to go through Westchester."

"All right," I said, "but how did you find this out?"

"Why, it looked to me Mawson's car had went too many miles if he was just going to see someone on Long Island. Then the guy in the garage said Mawson started for Boston. I found out where Landol lived, and we drove from where the car was found, past Landol's place, and back to Mawson's, and it made just the right distance. So I called headquarters and they had some Westchester cops search Landol's home and they found rope there like Mawson had been tied with. When Mawson got shot it broke his eyeglasses. I figure Landol picked up what pieces of glass he could find, but he was in a hurry and he missed some of 'em. The Westchester cops found those in Landol's living-room, because I'd said they was to look for 'em, and some of 'em was big enough so that Mawson's oculist could say it was the same prescription he had given Mawson."

"All very neat!" I stated, "but your explanation doesn't hold together because everything you did presupposes that you realized all along that it wasn't a gangster killed Mawson and suspected Landol might have done it; and you had no way of knowing that."

"Yeah? How about them knots Mawson was tied up with?"

"You said they didn't mean anything to you," I accused him indignantly.

"Sure they didn't. That's why I had to find out about 'em. I asked around, and it turned out they was surgeon's knots, the kind that doctors make in hospitals when they are doing operations."

"Nice work, O'Malley! You certainly had this case right."

"Yeah? Even a cop can't guess wrong all the time," he answered.

THREE BULLETS

Originally published in *Collier's*, April 15, 1933.

"This is another of them society murders," said O'Malley. "The dead guy was named Carlton, and he come in town from Long Island last night, for overnight, and he went to his folks' apartment. There wasn't nobody in the place except just him, because everybody, even the servants, are at the Long Island house, and they can't find that anybody came there. Still, he got knocked off. I guess I won't get much on it."

"How much have they got now?" I asked.

"Nothing, except that it looks like it might be a triangle case. This Carlton and another guy, named Roger Bassin, went with a lady named Mrs. Lessing. These are all young sporting folks, with plenty dough, that live partly in New York but mostly on Long Island and they ride fox hunting and have shooting parties and have dogs and horses, and you can't hardly tell who is married to who. Carlton and this guy Bassin was always good friends till they both got to going with Mrs. Lessing and wanted to marry her. Then they got less friendly. It was figured she would marry one of 'em, but nobody knew which. Well, she won't marry Carlton."

"Anything to connect Bassin with the murder?"

"Not yet. He was in Now York last night, and Mrs. Lessing was in town, too, but all these people come in separately. Here's where it happened."

We were at the Carlton apartment. It had more than a dozen rooms and it was full of cops. The biggest room was a sort of living-room-library.

"What they found out here?" O'Malley asked one of the officers.

"He was bumped off in that big room. Some shooting—three bullets not an inch apart! There wasn't nobody broke in here; whoever shot him come in after him, or was in here when he came. At night the hallboy runs the elevator; he didn't see nobody. Someone could walk up when he was in the elevator and walk down the same way."

We went around and looked at everything.

"What do you make of it, O'Malley?" I inquired.

"I wouldn't wonder if it was like that cop just said. Somebody came here and Carlton let 'em in, so I guess he knew 'em. Then they knocked him off."

There were some tiny shreds of crumpled newspaper on the carpet. O'Malley picked the biggest one up and smoothed it out. It was about as big as his thumb nail, so the words on it had no meaning.

"What's this?" he asked.

"I guess somebody tore up some newspaper," one of the officers answered.

O'Malley put the scrap of paper in his pocket.

"There ain't much to be got here," he said. "All these people that might have to do with this have been asked over to the station-house to talk with the inspector. We'll see what's doing there."

We went to the station-house and found it full of people.

"Nothing but limousines rolling up to this police station today," the desk officer remarked to us.

They had Bassin there and Mrs. Lessing and a man who proved to be Mr. Lessing and several chauffeurs and half a dozen servants. We didn't go into the room where the inspector was questioning them separately but talked with them while they waited outside. Bassin and Mrs. Lessing and Mr. Lessing all looked like people who lived much outdoors but stayed up too many nights.

"I've told all I know about this matter," Bassin told us irritably. "I dined at a club and went directly home. I didn't go out again. This morning the police came and told me Carlton was shot and asked if I had a small-caliber revolver. I replied that I belonged to a pistol club and had several pistols. They looked them over and took one away with them and asked me to come here."

"Did you know Carlton was going to be in town last night?"

"I did."

We went and talked with Mrs. Lessing. She was about twenty-four years old and pretty, but insipid-looking.

"Did you see Carlton yesterday?" O'Malley asked her.

"Yes; in the afternoon."

"Make any engagement to see him later? He went home but he just sat around like he might have been expecting somebody."

"No; I had no engagement with him."

"Mrs. Lessing knows nothing about this matter," Lessing said angrily. "She is entirely innocent and it is very unfortunate that she has been drawn into this."

"What's Lessing got to do with it?" I asked O'Malley.

"Not anything. Him and her are divorced but they're still friendly. When he heard she was asked here for questioning he came over to see if he could help her. There's always plenty guys want to help them baby-faced women."

Then a cop came out of the inspector's room and took Bassin back in for further questioning, and O'Malley followed them in but I stayed outside. O'Malley came out presently.

"Bassin tell anything more?" I asked.

"He didn't have to."

He had a photograph in his hand. The three bullets that killed Carlton had been photographed with three that the police had fired from Bassin's revolver; then the photograph had been cut and fitted together. The experts said that the markings made by the pistol barrel on all six bullets were exactly the same. There was no doubt that the bullets which killed Carlton had been fired from Bassin's revolver.

"That settles that!" I commented.

"Bassin don't say so. Says he hadn't touched or even seen the gun for a couple of weeks and he kept it locked up. Says if it was used it was done without his knowledge."

"That's ridiculous! He wants you to believe that someone entered his apartment, took the gun which was locked up, used it to kill Carlton, cleaned it, took it back to his apartment and locked it up again, all without his knowledge? Bassin might as well admit he did it."

"That's what these cops all think."

"Bassin had a motive, he knew Carlton would be in town, he is a marksman, and it was his gun."

"Sure. How about this?"

O'Malley took the scrap of newspaper from his pocket and smoothed it out. On one side it said "by Nassa," "ommunity actio," "for purpos," and the other side was part of an advertisement.

"These were all crumpled and torn up and scattered on the rug. They may mean something."

We left the station-house and parted. Bassin was arrested, and I didn't see O'Malley for a couple of days.

"I found what paper them pieces come from," he announced when I met him. "It said 'Nassa,' so I thought that might mean Nassau County and it might be some paper published on Long Island. Well, it was."

He had a copy of the issue from which the fragment had been torn. It came out of a paragraph about community work in Nassau County.

"I don't see," I said, "what that article could have to do with the murder."

"It ain't got nothing. I wanted to find out who subscribed to that paper. Well, Carlton didn't, and Bassin and Mrs. Lessing don't. Some guys that belong to the shooting club do."

We drove out on Long Island to the shooting club. A Negro attendant showed us around.

"Mr. Bassin a good pistol shot?" O'Malley asked him.

"Yassah. Very fine shot."

"How about Mr. Carlton?"

"He was good. Mrs. Lessing, too."

"How about Lessing?"

"Mr. Lessing don't shoot no revolvah. He shoot clay pigeons. Mr. Lessing say he can't hit a barn doah with a revolvah, can't hit a bale of hay. He hit it, though."

"Hit what?"

"Bale of hay."

"Let's get this: Mr. Bassin and Mr. Lessing were talking about pistol shooting and Mr. Lessing took Mr. Bassin's revolver and fired it at a bale of hay?"

"Yassah. And plenty times he hit it."

"When was this?"

"Two, three weeks ago."

We got back in the car and went to look for Lessing. Since his divorce he had maintained quarters in several clubs. One was a golf club. He wasn't there but they said he was expected, so we waited. His servant let us wait in his rooms. They were luxurious. There were riding and golfing things about and there were several shotguns.

"Did Lessing subscribe to that newspaper?" I asked.

"That's right."

Then Lessing came in.

"The inspector wants to see you," O'Malley said.

We drove back to New York.

"Where were you, Mr. Lessing, the night Carlton got killed?" O'Malley asked him, as we started.

"I was on Long Island."

"You're lucky. If you'd happened to drive into town that night, and maybe took a bag of golf clubs with you, you might have been suspected."

"Possibly. No imbecility on the part of the police would surprise me."

"Yeah?" O'Malley answered. "Well, I'm going to be dumb enough to arrest you for this murder."

We took him to headquarters.

"See here, O'Malley," I said, after we had left him, "Lessing apparently committed this murder, but I don't get it."

"You better clean your eyeglasses. This Lessing is a guy that couldn't get along with his wife and can't get along without her, and he wasn't willing nobody else should have her. She was going with Carlton and Bassin and would probably marry one of 'em, and Lessing figured if one of 'em got killed and she thought the other one did it, she wouldn't marry either of 'em.

"He wanted some bullets that had been fired from Bassin's revolver. These guys all belonged to the shooting club, so that was easy. Lessing fired the revolver at a bale of hay, and afterward he got the bullets."

"Then what?"

"Then he took the shot out of a shotgun shell and put three bullets in place of it, packing 'em in tight with newspaper. When he shot Carlton, it blew the newspaper into little pieces all over the place."

"Very neat!" I appreciated. "But Lessing took a long chance of someone's seeing him with that gun."

"You won't ever get smart. Didn't you hear what I said to him? He carried the shotgun in a golf bag."

"A nice piece of work!" I gloated.

"You think I done a good job? Well, I guess some of these other cops will get a lot of credit out of it," he answered.

THE MIND READER

Originally published in *Collier's*, July 22, 1933m.

"Several guys," said O'Malley, "got knocked off, all in the same neighbor-hood. They was strangers that come to town with money. Now another guy got pushed over, so they put me on the case. Cosimo his name was, and he come from Rochester. It happened in a rooming-house. We won't solve this because everybody that knows anything is afraid to tell it. It's just bad luck my getting this case."

"Have you got any lead at all?" I asked.

"The guy that runs the rooming-house knows more than he is telling. He says if someone came in with Cosimo he didn't see him. You can't blame him; he's an honest guy himself but liable to be shoved across if he says different."

"It sounds like a tough case."

"You said it."

The rooming-house was four stories with a high basement. People were gos-siping on doorsteps all around but not on this one. A uniformed cop sat in the doorway reading a newspaper.

"Anyone around this place?" O'Malley asked him.

"I'm the only tenant. The birds that live here," the cop explained, "got no more baggage than a second shirt. When this happened each of 'em took his ex-tra shirt and moved out before the police could get here. They got the proprietor at the station-house."

"You got his keys?"

"Yeah, I got those."

"I guess we ought to look around a little."

We followed the cop upstairs. The murder room was on the second floor. It held a bed, a dresser and one chair. There was nothing else in the room except an empty red-wine bottle and two glasses on the window sill.

"They took everything this bird had," the cop informed us. "His clothes and baggage. Domenico says the bird come in here alone. Would a bird that was alone drink out of two glasses, stab himself in the back and carry out his baggage afterward? There ain't no fingerprints on them glasses. They left the knife here."

"Is Domenico the man that runs the place?" I asked.

"That's right."

"What do you make of it, O'Malley?"

"It's like I said it was. The robbed guy got killed so there would be no wit-ness. It's some kind of murder ring. They seen this Cosimo had money and got acquainted with him and one or more of 'em come here with him to his room. Nobody will talk, so we got no way to tell who done the killing. It might be someone from outside or some of those that lived here."

We went all through the building looking at everything. Some of the rooms were locked but the cop unlocked them with his bunch of keys. There were things scattered about such as men would leave who were departing hurriedly. On the top floor one room was different. It was rather luxuriously furnished and the bureau drawers were filled with a man's things and his clothes were hanging in the closet. The owner's name on the tailor's label in the clothes said: "Jos. Di-Palda."

"Whoever DiPalda is," I remarked, "he is apparently expecting to come back here."

We found nothing else. When we came out of the building one of the prettiest girls I ever saw, about seventeen years old, was standing on the sidewalk waiting for us.

"What's on your mind, girlie?" O'Malley asked her.

"I would wish to know what you are doing with Domenico."

* * * *

People on doorsteps near and on the sidewalk were listening. One of them was a big man with two pin-points of mustache.

"She has interest in Domenico," he informed us suavely, "because he is our friend, but there is no use asking policemen anything, Philomena."

"You got that much right, fellow, anyway," O'Malley told him. "Any of you people know anything about this homicide?"

They didn't. We went around and questioned people in all the neighboring buildings. Sometimes we didn't question them, because when they saw us coming they disappeared before we got to them. Nobody knew anything. They couldn't even tell us the name of anyone who lived in Domenico's rooming-house.

"Well, there you got it!" O'Malley declared finally. "This murder might as well happened in some statue hall in the Metropolitan Museum. What's the use questioning people whose eyes and ears and tongues are made of marble? You get no answers. I knew we wouldn't get nothing. Let's quit and go to a show and I'll report I couldn't get no clue."

I didn't feel like going to a show.

"See you tomorrow at the station-house," I told him.

I met him the next day.

"How was the show?" I asked.

"Swell. They had a dame there that read guys' minds. I came away for fear she might read mine. This is the knife that Cosimo guy got killed with."

The knife had been made out of a file. It had been wrapped in paper so that it could not be seen to be a knife and had been used without taking the paper off.

"Not much chance of tracing that," I decided.

"Not any. They got Domenico here still, but now they got to let him go."

We went in where they had Domenico. He was a small man about sixty years old, with white hair, and he had a pleasant, determined face.

"How is it you get nothing out of this guy?" O'Malley asked the officers.

Domenico answered for them: "They get notting out of dees guy because he don't know notting."

When they let him go we went out of the station-house with him. It was plain he didn't want to be seen with us but there was nothing he could do about it. He was going home. When we had gone a few blocks we came to a small theater which had motion pictures and vaudeville. A sign outside said, "Madame Fortuna appears here afternoon and evening. She reads the trouble in your mind and answers it. Consult her between performances."

"We'll go in here," O'Malley stated.

Domenico didn't want to go in but he couldn't help himself. Some people were waiting to consult Madame Fortuna but they let us in ahead of them. She was a stout middle-aged woman, very blond, in a black dress, who sat in a room hung everywhere with red.

"I got a guy here to get his mind read," O'Malley told her.

Domenico was startled. Then he was frightened.

"Nossir, nossir!" he cried, and he started for the door.

We dragged him back.

"I'll see what I can get," Madame Fortuna agreed. She shut her eyes and covered them with her hands. "I get something tragic in this guy's mind," she declared after a moment. "Is it—murder? Yes, it's murder he is thinking about."

"Keep on, lady, you're doing fine," O'Malley urged her.

"It was somewhere in a room." She described the room. It was a good description of the murder room. "Two men are there. I can't be sure—there may be more of 'em. There may be three or four. A big man is in his shirt sleeves. He and another one drink wine. Now the other one stands behind the big man. He makes a signal and then stabs him."

"That's swell!" O'Malley commended. "Does this guy's mind give you any picture of the one that done the killing?"

"Sure it does. It gives a real good picture. He is about twenty years old and tall—six feet, I guess; black hair, dark eyes and say, boy! that guy is handsome. He's got a curved scar about half an inch long under his lower lip but it don't disfigure him any."

"Who would that be, Domenico?" O'Malley asked.

Domenico was very white. "Not nobody!" he cried excitedly. "No, no, no, no! I don't know nobody like that."

We went outside. Domenico was anxious and uneasy. When we let him go he scurried down the street.

"You aren't serious about this, O'Malley," I objected. "You don't believe that woman described the killer to you?"

"She described the room and she had never seen it, and we got nothing else but this to go on."

"You're nuts!"

"Yeah? That's been thought before. And I don't have to go searching for the guy she told about; I know where he is."

* * * *

On the way we picked up a plain-clothes cop and then went to a hotel. O'Malley knew the room. We knocked at it and a remarkably good-looking young man, who had been poring over a heavy book, opened the door. He was black-haired and had a half-inch scar under his lower lip.

"Come on, DiPalda," O'Malley told him. "They want to see you at the station-house."

We let the plain-clothes cop take DiPalda to the station-house while we hurried to Domenico's.

"What now?" the officer on post there asked us.

"We got a lead."

Domenico was peeking at us through the crack of his kitchen door. He followed us when we went upstairs. We hadn't searched the top-floor room before but now we searched it thoroughly. In a dresser drawer, hidden under some shirts, we found a file exactly like the one the knife had been made from, wrapped in the same kind of paper. Among the clothes hanging in the closet was a brown suit which had a button missing; some of the cloth had been torn out with the button.

"Fine!" said O'Malley. "Here's the button the dead guy pulled off the killer's coat and had clutched in his fingers."

He took a brown button from his pocket and held it against the coat. It matched the other buttons and the torn cloth fitted.

"No, no!" Domenico yelled. "You are a beeg liar! Dees dead guy don't have no button in his fingers. You don't arres' dees Joseph!"

"He feels bad," O'Malley explained to me, "because DiPalda is his grandson."

We went back to the station-house, but we stopped for supper on the way, so Domenico beat us to it. He was in the captain's room when we got there, and the very pretty girl who had spoken to us outside Domenico's was watching the closed door anxiously.

"This guy inside spill anything?" O'Malley asked the desk lieutenant.

"I'll say. I don't know what happened to him but he come here talking plenty."

* * * *

O'Malley went into the captain's room. I waited. There was a lot of activity around the station-house. After a while O'Malley came out again and we both waited. Finally an officer came in bringing a suitcase. Then another one came with a watch and some clothes. Then a whole group of cops came in bringing three sullen men. One of them was the big man with the pinpoint mustache who had spoken to us about his "friend" Domenico.

"Soboni, Oscani, Morino," the lieutenant checked them off.

"Well, saps," O'Malley said to them, "you let life out of several parties; how you going to feel when it happens to yourself?"

"I don't get this, O'Malley," I complained.

"Why not? You was along with me. This Domenico knew something and was afraid to tell it, so I figured the way to make him talk was to make him still more afraid of something else. Then, at the show, I seen that mind-reader lady. This Joe DiPalda is a fine kid and is studying to be a doctor and is engaged to that girl Philomena; and the old man is crazy over both of 'em. When this killing happened the first thing Domenico done was to get his grandson out of the place, so the boy wouldn't even get the blot on him of police questioning.

"I never seen DiPalda, but some other cops give me a description of him and told me where he was. I fixed it with the mind reader to describe Joe as the one that done the killing. I figured that would make Domenico talk.

"Domenico knew the file and button was a plant, but he was scared about the mind-reading. I guess he thought I believed DiPalda was guilty and that we planted the evidence because I was determined to convict him. There wasn't nothing Domenico wouldn't risk to keep his grandson from being charged with murder; so he beat it to the station-house. When he got here he couldn't prove his grandson wasn't guilty without telling what he knew. Domenico didn't see who done the murder. What he seen was Oscani and Morino coming down the stairs afterward with Cosimo's suitcase. Those two always palled with Sobini, and Domenico figured the three of 'em was the murder mob. They had pawned Cosimo's things."

"It was a remarkable piece of psychology, O'Malley, and you ought to get big credit for it."

"Say, I hope it don't get mentioned outside the station-house. Would I want to get known as a guy that planted evidence? I got troubles enough in this police department without that!"

THROUGH THE CABIN WINDOW

Originally published in *Collier's*, July 29, 1933.

"This murder happened on a coal barge," said O'Malley. "The dead guy's name is Captain Solan. One guy lives on these boats and so they call him 'captain' and he has a deckhand to help him. Solan's deckhand's name is Alshuler. Well, Alshuler says he was uptown to spend the evening and he come back about midnight and the captain was in the cabin, dead. His head had been beat in with an iron bolt. You can't never find out about these waterfront killings because too many times they get done by someone that never even seen the guy before; if you do find out it don't get you nothing because generally nobody cares if the guy got killed or didn't. This Solan's wife was dead and he didn't have no relatives. Alshuler says he never wrote no letters."

"Have they any idea as to the motive?"

"Right now they think it was robbery. The captain had a couple of bond coupons in his pocket. They was due to be paid yesterday, the first of the month. Well, that was Sunday so he couldn't cash 'em, but he couldn't have sold the bonds without the coupons, so he must still have had 'em. They can't find no bonds."

"Who do they think did it?"

"Some people think it was Alshuler."

We went to see Captain Solan. He had been a big man with white hair, between sixty and seventy years old. He had a Statue of Liberty tattooed on one forearm and a warship on the other. Under the statue were the letters C. S. and under the warship J. P.

"What do you suppose the letters stand for, O'Malley?" I inquired.

"C. S. might stand for Charles Solan. I don't know about J. P. Well, we got to see Alshuler, but he won't tell us nothing."

We went to headquarters and saw Alshuler. He was a weasel-faced little man with shifty eyes.

"You told everything you know about this homicide?" O'Malley asked him.

"Sure. Because I don't know nothing. I was uptown and I come back. That was at midnight. I looked in the cabin and the captain was dead and so I called the cops."

"You and the captain ever have any trouble between you?"

"No; we never had no trouble."

"He's not telling all he knows, O'Malley," I decided.

"You're right in that, but they got another witness."

The other witness was named Tadden. He was a good-looking young fellow, twenty-two years old, with an honest face.

"You tell us exactly what you told them other cops," O'Malley directed him.

"Well, I work on a barge. Our barge was tied up outside of Captain Solan's. A little before midnight I started to go home and I had to cross Solan's barge to get to the wharf. So I glanced in at Solan's window and he was in the cabin. He was washing his hands."

"You know this Captain Solan pretty well?"

"Sure."

"You ever knew of him having trouble with anybody?"

"He wasn't the kind that ever caused no trouble. There was no harm in the old boy except he bored you stiff talking about when he was in the Navy."

"When you seen him through the cabin window did you speak to him?"

"No; I just went on to the wharf."

"O. K. Then what happened?"

"When I was about half a dozen blocks up the street I met Alshuler on his way back to the barge. That's all."

"How long would you say it would have been from when you seen the captain to when Alshuler would have got back to the barge?"

"Maybe fifteen minutes."

"Well, O'Malley," I said, "that doesn't leave much time for the murder to be done by anyone but Alshuler."

"You think he done it?"

"I've thought so from the first minute I saw him."

"You might be right. So now we got more trouble—we got to go look at the barge."

The barge was in the East River. Several barges were tied up abreast and the one we wanted was next against the wharf. As Tadden had told us, anyone who wanted to get ashore from one of the others had to walk across its deck. There was a pile of long iron bolts on the wharf like the one Solan had been killed with, which we had seen at headquarters, and a uniformed cop was sitting in an arm-chair on the deck. When we went down into the cabin, the cop followed us.

I didn't like the cabin very well. There was blood over everything and papers were scattered all around.

"The plain-clothes guys that were here ahead of you searched this place," the cop informed us.

There was a picture of a very pretty woman on the cabin wall, who, we decided, must have been Solan's wife. We examined all the papers but found nothing of importance. Some of the papers related to a steamship company that Solan had once worked for, and others, before that, to his service in the navy. There was a photograph of two youngsters in the naval uniform of enlisted men.

"Would you think the tallest of these guys was Solan?" O'Malley asked me.

"He looks like it."

He put the picture in his pocket. "Where did Alshuler sleep?" he asked the cop.

The cop showed us and O'Malley searched that place too. I sat on the bunk and watched him. Then I felt something lumpy in the mattress of the bunk and I turned the mattress over and felt in it. It was a package wrapped in oilskin, which contained ten bonds, and two of them were the ones from which the coupons had been cut that had been found in Solan's pockets.

"Here's your case, O'Malley," I declared exultantly. "Alshuler killed the old man and took the bonds and hid them. Probably he'd had some drinks uptown. When he got back and looked in the cabin he saw Solan handling the bonds. He stepped back on the wharf and got the iron bolt and killed the old man and took the bonds and hid them. Then he called the police."

"If he done the murder he'd ought to have had some blood on him."

"He changed his clothes and dropped the other ones overboard before he notified the police."

We went back into the larger cabin.

"You act like you was washing your hands," O'Malley directed me, "while I go up above and see if I can see you the way Tadden said."

I went and pretended to wash my hands. It was a tiny window and close down to the deck.

"Could you see me?" I asked when he came back downstairs.

"Sure I could see you. I could see your hands and arms and shoulders and part of your body and a little of your chin. I couldn't see no more, though."

We took the bonds to headquarters and gave them to the inspector and he sent for Alshuler.

"What have you got to say to this, Eddie?" the inspector asked.

Alshuler studied us with his weasel face and shifting eyes, and seemed to think. He looked like some small, bloodthirsty, cornered animal.

"Sure I took the bonds," he said at last, "after I found the old man dead. He didn't have no folks and they belonged to me as much as anybody, and I knew where he kept 'em. I suppose you think I'd ought to have left 'em for you cops."

"Smart lad!" the chief informed him.

We went outside.

"You made quick work of that case, O'Malley," I congratulated him.

"Yeah. I didn't hear the inspector say I was taken off of it, so I guess I'm still on it, and I'd like to find out some more about this Captain Solan."

"What's to find out?" I asked. "He was in the Navy and then with a steamship company and when he got old he got a job aboard a coal barge."

"Yeah, I guess I won't find out no more than just that," he answered.

* * * *

We parted and I didn't see him for a couple of days and then I met him walking along Spring Street.

"Anything more about Solan?" I inquired.

"No; not about him. His life was like you said. But now I got to take a little sea voyage down to the lower bay."

I went along. A police launch with a couple of plain-clothes men and a uniformed officer was waiting for us and we put-putted down the harbor to the lower bay, where a dingy tramp was rolling at her anchors in the tide.

"You got a man aboard named James Park?" O'Malley asked the skipper.

"We have."

A seaman took us down below to where a big, white-haired man was lying in a bunk.

"Get your coat on, Jim," O'Malley said to him. "We want you."

He got up and put on his coat. A Statue of Liberty was tattooed on one of his forearms and a warship on the other. Under the statue were the letters J. P. and under the warship C. S.

We took him to headquarters and Park and O'Malley went into the inspector's room but I stayed outside. After a while the two came out together.

"Park killed him. You tell it, Park."

"Why," Park explained, without much hesitation, "I and this Charlie Solan, from boys up, were pals. We went into the Navy together and figured we'd stick together all our lives. We did everything together and got tattooed alike, with our two initials put on both of us. Then I got married. That didn't seem to make any difference; Charlie and me and my wife all went around together. Then he shipped on a freighter and I never heard from him again.

"A little after that my wife left me and I couldn't ever find out why or where she went. I never connected her and him, and I didn't see him again for about twenty years. Ten days ago I got into New York on that tramp from Rio de Janeiro and in the harbor I saw a man on a barge that looked like him. I figured to look my old pal up and was mighty glad to see him; but when I found him, there was my wife's picture looking at me on his cabin wall.

"That was the first I knew that when she left me she had gone to him. I taxed him with it and he told it plain enough. It was all old stuff to him, but to me it was like it had just happened. It all come over me how them two had made a fool out of me for twenty years, and so I knocked him off. I'm glad I did."

They locked him up.

* * * *

"That's all very well, O'Malley," I objected, "but how did you find this out?"

"Well, this crime didn't look right to me from the first. I couldn't think a little sneaky guy like that Alshuler would knock off a big guy like Captain Solan; and if he did, he wouldn't have sent for the police; he'd have lit out. The hardest kind of crime to solve is one where there's a plain reason who did it and why it was done, but the real reason and person is one that nobody ever thinks of. Tadden was honest in saying he seen Solan on the barge just before Alshuler got there; he thought he did. But that didn't hardly leave time for the murder to take place if Alshuler didn't do it.

"Then I looked at you through the cabin window washing your hands and I could only see a part of you. So maybe Tadden hadn't really seen Solan but someone he thought was him, and that guy would be the murderer and he was washing the blood off of him when Tadden seen him. Of course I didn't have no hunch that the two had been tattooed alike, which was what fooled Tadden; but he must have seen somebody about Solan's age and in some ways like him. The only way to find that guy was to dig up Solan's past life.

"We found some papers showing where he'd been and a picture of two young guys in navy uniform, one of whom was him. I asked around among a lot of old seafarin' guys who the other one was and he turned out to be named Park. So then I traced down Park. If he was anywheres near New York last Sunday he was open to suspicion, and I found he'd got in New York a week before from Rio de Janeiro. So then we pinched him. . . ."

"It was a wonderful piece of police work," I commended him, "and Alshuler owes you a lot of gratitude. You certainly saved him from the chair."

"I won't get no thanks from Alshuler. That kind of guy wouldn't think he owed nothing to nobody even if you made him police commissioner."

SPILLED PERFUME

Originally published in *Collier's*, September 30, 1933.

"Now we got a hotel murder," said O'Malley. "These are some people named Mr. and Mrs. Wester, of Philadelphia, and they come to the hotel. So a bellhop showed them to Room 1215. Then the next morning the maid come to do up the room and she knocked and got no answer; so then she went in. The guy was on the bed with his head knocked in."

"Where was his wife?" I asked.

"They don't know what become of his wife. The last they seen of her was the afternoon before when she went out to do some shopping."

"Is that all they know about it?"

"I don't know yet what they know. Here's the hotel."

It was a big hotel. Everything was going on as though nothing had happened. We found two plain-clothes men in the hotel office.

"You boys know anything about this case?" O'Malley asked them.

"Sure. We got wires from Philadelphia. This Wester had a grocery in Philly. Well, he wanted to get married, so he advertised for a wife, and a woman answered. So he used to go week-ends to see her in Atlantic City. But she didn't want to live in Philly after they got married, so he sold his store for fourteen thousand dollars. Yesterday morning he wired his friends that they got married. This was his wedding trip."

"He didn't get a very long one. Did he have the dough on him when he come here?"

"We don't know about the dough. What we got to do now is find his wife."

"What do you know about the lady?"

"Nothing. None of his friends had ever met her."

"What does she look like?"

"The hotel says she wasn't very big and had black hair. That's all they know."

"You boys got a life job if you're going to try to find her with no more than that. There's five hundred thousand dames in this town that answer that description."

They had a photograph of the man as he had been found. He had no coat or vest on. He was a big man with sandy, straight-up hair.

"Well," O'Malley said, "we won't find out anything but we got to go look at the room."

* * * *

An assistant manager of the hotel went up with us. A floor-clerk at a desk faced us when we got out of the elevator. All the odd-numbered rooms were to the right of the clerk's desk and the even ones to the left. There was a uniformed officer in Room 1215. A man's suitcase was open and some of his things were on a dresser. His coat and vest were hanging in a closet.

"How was this?" O'Malley asked the officer.

"The medical office thinks the bird was asleep when he got knocked off. They think what done it was a hammer. They didn't find no hammer. He was all right just before his wife went out to do her shopping because this room called for cracked ice and a bellhop brought it up and the wife said don't make any noise because her husband was asleep. The bellhop seen him and he was just asleep; he wasn't dead. The wife went out only a couple of minutes later. The door was locked and the room key was on the dresser. The door locks itself when it gets shut."

"What do you think of it, O'Malley?" I inquired.

"I got no idea."

"My idea," said the cop, "is that his wife knocked him off."

"Yeah?" said O'Malley. "Where's this lady's baggage? She didn't go on a wedding trip without no baggage?"

I was surprised. I hadn't noticed before that there was no evidence of a woman's occupancy in the room.

"She had a small brown suitcase," the manager informed us. "We don't know what became of it. She didn't take it with her and it wasn't carried out by anyone else or we should have a record of it. There's a floor-clerk on every floor who makes note of everything carried out of the rooms, or if it is taken down the service elevator or service stairs the porter has a record of it. It wasn't here when the murdered man was found."

"Did this dead guy ask for any particular room in the hotel?"

"Not that, exactly. He asked for a room on the east side of the house on the eleventh or twelfth floor."

"You don't think," I remarked derisively, "that he asked for this particular room in order to be murdered in it?"

"He might."

There was a sweet and pungent aroma in the room.

"This lady used strong perfume," O'Malley observed. "I guess she spilled some of it."

He went and smelled of a stained spot on the dresser cover. I smelled it too. The scent was distinctive and I didn't remember meeting it before.

O'Malley cut the stained spot out of the dresser cover and put it in an envelope.

"Well, we ain't found much here," he decided.

Then we went back to the hotel office because O'Malley wanted to find out who had checked out of the hotel. There were quite a lot of them. O'Malley crossed off a number of the names. The manager knew some of the others as frequent guests of the hotel and O'Malley crossed those off too.

"You got a record which of these folks had trunks?" They had; and O'Malley marked them off too. There were three names left.

"I don't suppose you keep what comes out of the wastebaskets in these rooms?" he questioned.

"We do until we are sure the guest has not thrown anything away which he will ask for afterward."

A clerk brought some big envelopes. They were dated and marked with room numbers. There was no writing in them or anything that seemed to me to have importance. In the envelope marked 1231 there was the paper cover of a packet of matches with a telephone number written on it.

"What kind of a guy was in Room 1231?" O'Malley asked.

They remembered him as a big man with blond hair, well dressed. He had been in the hotel a couple of days and had checked out the afternoon before, more than twelve hours before the discovery of the murder. His baggage had been a big suitcase.

"There's plenty guys in this town that could be described like that," O'Malley commented.

He called up the telephone number to see what it was and it proved to be a church on Long Island.

"Nothing in that," he said, disappointedly. "Well, we done a lot of work here and we have got nowhere. I'll let you know if anything turns up."

We left the hotel and the next day he called me up.

"You want to go out on Long Island?"

I met him at the station and we took a train out to Long Beach. A couple of plain-clothes men were on the same train with us but they didn't speak to us or we to them. When we got to Long Beach we walked around and watched the bathers. A little before dinner-time we went to a café. The two plainclothes men who had come out on the train with us were there but they didn't seem to notice us.

"This is the kind of perfume that lady used," O'Malley remarked to me.

He produced a little bottle and uncorked it.

"Try some on your handkerchief." Wave it around and see how nice it smells."

He spilled nearly half the contents of the bottle on my handkerchief and the scent filled the place. Most of the men and women turned and looked at us. I wondered what kind of people they thought we were. One man didn't look at us. He was a big man with blond hair and he seemed very nervous. He kept wiping the sweat off his temples with his napkin and finally he got up and went out. We stayed where we were but the two plain-clothes men went out after him. A little later we went out too. One of the plain-clothes men was standing down the street and we followed him and found the other one around a corner.

"In there," the second man said to us, jerking his head toward a little bunga-low.

The two plain-clothes men went around to the rear of the bungalow and we waited in front, but we didn't go in. After a while a small woman with black hair came up from the beach in a bathing suit and went into the bungalow; so we went in. The woman was swiftly packing a small brown suitcase and the man was throwing things into another huge one.

"What is the meaning of this intrusion?" the man demanded when he saw us.

"We got an idea you two are going to be pinched for murder, fellow."

The woman ran swiftly to the rear door, but the two plain-clothes men were coming in that way. They watched us uneasily while we searched the bungalow. We found a small packet of bills tacked to the under side of a dresser drawer. Then we found another in the back of a framed picture. Later we found some more. When we had all the packets they made fourteen thousand dollars.

"Fair enough, buddy," O'Malley told the man. "Is this lady your wife?"

"She is."

"How was all this, O'Malley?" I demanded, as we sat looking at the ocean and waiting for the police wagon.

"Why, it was a murder trap," he answered. "When this Wester advertised to get married, this lady and her husband fixed it up that she would answer him. Their idea was to kill him for his dough. She met him in Atlantic City, where he wouldn't know anything about her except the story she told him, and where she wouldn't meet none of his friends that could recognize her after. She got him to sell his store.

"They got married and come to New York, with him bringing the money, and they went to that hotel where her husband had took a room a couple of days before and was waiting for 'em. She got Wester to ask for a room near where her husband's room was. When they was in the room she got him to lay down for a nap while she went out to shop. After he was asleep she went to Room 1231 and give her husband the key and told him it was O. K. and Wester was asleep, and then she walked out of the hotel. Her husband went to the room and knocked Wester off and took the dough and left the key inside the room and went back to his own room. Then he checked out."

"I understood most of that," I said, "but what became of her baggage?"

O'Malley got up and put the small suitcase inside the big one. It still left room for some clothes.

"I see," I said. Her husband, after the murder, took her suitcase to his room and it was carried out inside his bigger one. But how did you trace them down?"

"Why, she was a little woman and Wester was a big man and I figured she couldn't take the chance to murder him; so someone was working with her. But there wasn't any indication she was working with someone in the hotel, so probably it was a guest. But it wasn't a guest in an even-numbered room because to get back and forth to that odd-numbered room he would have had to pass the floor-clerk. So I was looking for a guest that had checked out from an odd-numbered room near the twelfth floor who had a bag big enough for a small suitcase to go into it. I found a guy like that had had Room 1231."

"Very neat," I complimented him. "Then what?"

"These people figured to leave no trace who they were, but there is usually something if a cop can find it. She had spilled some of her perfume and the guy in 1231 had threw away a match folder with a telephone number on it. I called the number up and it turned out a church—so that didn't mean nothing. It wasn't till after that I thought how crooks sometimes write a number backwards so it is plain to them but not to other people. So then I called the phone number backward and it was a Long Beach café.

"There ain't no telephone in this bungalow, so I guess if him or his wife wanted to get the other one they had to telephone this café. That meant that they used this café sometimes. I figured if one of 'em happened to be in there and a cop spilled some of the perfume around that she used in the murder room they would get nervous and maybe pick themselves out for us. He knew I was a cop all right. There was only one guy that perfume meant anything to except just foolery, but to him it meant the cops had spotted him. It was just luck we got him the first time we tried it. I had got plenty of the stuff and I was prepared to keep spilling it around at different times until I was sure neither him nor her was there."

"It certainly worked," I said. "You picked two people out of about six million with very little to go on."

"Yeah, I was lucky. Probably the next case I'm on the guy I'm after will come up and ask me the time of day and I won't know it's him."

HELP FROM UNCLE SAM

Originally published in *Collier's*, October 28, 1933.

"This case," said O'Malley, "is a jeweler got pushed over. We won't solve it. Paden & Company the firm is called. Well, this Mr. Paden opened up the store this morning and some holdups came in and knocked him off."

"Just how was it done?" I asked.

"A guy come in as if he was a customer. Then two more guys come in. So Paden saw it was a holdup and he tried to shut the safe, and then they shot him. These were experienced holdups and worked by the clock, so we won't catch them. The precinct cops pinched a guy named Enbrook."

"What's the evidence?"

"He had been hanging round the store. Experienced guys don't work unless they know what they are going to get by it and they think he sized the place up for 'em."

We stopped at the station-house to see the man who had been pinched. He was about twenty-four years old and wasn't bad-looking. He wouldn't tell anything about himself.

"You deny you was in with this bunch that knocked the jeweler off?" O'Malley demanded of him.

"Certainly I deny it."

"Then what were you hanging round the store for?"

"I've got a right to go anywhere I want."

"We won't get nothing out of this guy," O'Malley decided. "Probably we won't learn anything at the store, but we got to look at it. We'll see the shot guy first."

We went and looked at Paden. He was a little man, round-shouldered and white-haired, about sixty years old. I was surprised that he had resisted the robbers. Afterward we went to the store. It was a small shop, in the north end of Manhattan. There were a lot of cops there and a clerk and one of the prettiest red-headed girls I ever saw, who proved to be Miss Paden. She had been crying.

"Got anything on this?" O'Malley asked the officers.

"We got a hat."

They showed it to us. "It ain't Paden's hat because his is hanging in the closet, so maybe it belonged to one of the holdups."

"What did they get?" O'Malley asked.

"About $40,000." The cops had a list furnished by the insurance company.

"You know anything about this Enbrook, Miss Paden?" O'Malley asked the girl.

"Yes; I met him at the beach. Afterward he came to the store sometimes. I thought he came here to see me, but now the police think that he was finding out things for the robbers."

"Your dad always open up the store?"

"No; Mr. Malling usually opened it."

"Who's he?"

"Father's partner. Father wasn't very active in the business. Mr. Malling was hit by a taxicab last night and is in the hospital. Father went over to see him last night but Mr. Malling was unconscious."

"Well," O'Malley decided, "I guess there are enough cops here to find out about that hat. We might go see Malling."

We went to the hospital. They let us see him. Malling was a big man about thirty-five years old and very handsome.

"How come," O'Malley asked him, "you got hit?"

"I don't know a thing about it. I was crossing the street and the next I knew I was in the hospital. It doesn't matter about me. This is terrible, gentlemen, about Gerald Paden. He gave me my start in life."

"What time this accident happen?"

"It must have been about one o'clock this morning. I had been to an after-theater supper with some friends."

"What restaurant?"

"O'Connel's."

"You know anything about Enbrook, Mr. Malling?"

"Only that he came to the store several times."

"We'll see the bird that hit this guy," O'Malley said after we had left the hospital.

The police had the taxi driver's name and address and the number of his cab. We found him presently. He was a tough young fellow.

"How was that accident?" O'Malley asked him.

"I can't tell you a thing. I never seen him till he stepped in front of the cab."

"This seems to be getting pretty plain, O'Malley," I volunteered.

"Yeah? How so?"

"It's too much coincidence for one partner to be hit by a taxi and the other one murdered the next morning, unless there was some connection. Malling usually opened the store, but when he didn't Paden opened it. Malling's a big, courageous man and they preferred not to tackle him. The taxi driver got Malling out of the way for them. Enbrook may have been the tip-off man; I don't know. The way to solve this is to find out who the taxi man associates with."

"You always got ideas. I'm going to make out my report and go and see a picture."

"What are you going to report?"

"Report I found out nothing."

I saw him the next day.

"Get anything on that taxi man?" I asked.

"I ain't got much on anybody. I might get something now."

We went to a West Side apartment building and he rang a bell. The card beside the bell said "I. Walger." It didn't mean anything to me. He rang a dozen times but got no answer.

"Not home," he said in disappointment.

There were some letters in the mail box over the name, and O'Malley peered it them through the little glass panel.

"I'd like to know what's in them letters, but a guy that robs the U. S. mail gets himself in trouble. You better ****o round the corner."

I went around the corner and waited and in a few minutes he rejoined me, throwing away a piece of wire.

"What was in the letters?" I asked.

"What letters? If you don't want the government to put me in the can, I wouldn't talk about letters. I think****better telephone."

We stopped at a drug store while he telephoned.

"Did you ever go to a hotel and register as John V. Huber?" he asked when he came out again.

"No, I never even heard of the name."

"Well, it might be a good thing to try."

"Not for me," I said, "unless I know why I'm doing it."

"You might not be useful to me if you knew."

We went to the Times Square district and he pointed out to me a side-street hotel.

"Does John V. Huber come from anywhere in particular?" I asked.

"He might come from Newark."

He left me and I went into the hotel and registered as John V. Huber, Newark.

"There's a package here for you, Mr. Huber," the clerk informed me.

He gave me a small, square package and a bell-hop showed me to my room. I didn't know what this was all about, or what was expected of me, and I just sat and looked at the unopened package. Then a knock came at the door and I opened it and let in O'Malley.

"You done that fine," he complimented me when he saw the package.

I was glad of that, but I didn't know what I'd done. We opened the package and found a smaller one inside it, and opened that one and found a handful of un-set diamonds.

"Maybe now," I demanded, "you'll tell me what this is all about."

"Sure I'll tell you. But first I got a piece of news for you. They got them holdups. Them smart cops traced down that hat."

We went to the station-house and looked at them—three sullen, hard-faced young men. They wouldn't talk.

"Malling will be glad they're caught," I stated.

"Yeah. We'll go tell him."

We went to the hospital. Malling was up and dressed.

"You look like they're going to let you out of here," O'Malley observed.

"Yes. I'm bruised, but fortunately suffered no greater injury."

"We got the guys that done that murder. Do you feel able to go over to the station with us?"

"I'm not likely to recognize them, but I'll be glad to give you any help I can."

"We don't need no help. We want you as accessory to the murder."

Malling turned white. "Why, that's ridiculous! I was unconscious when it happened."

"Sure you were. If you hadn't been unconscious there wouldn't have been no murder."

Malling fainted, but he was all right in a few minutes and we took him to the station-house. The police had a flashy blond girl there named Irene Walger. They locked her up too.

"I'm all at sea on this, O'Malley," I told him.

"Yeah? Malling used to be Paden's clerk. A couple of years ago, when Paden wanted partly to retire, he made him his partner. Malling couldn't stand prosperity. He began stepping out, gambled and went around with women and got himself in debt. So he got the idea to have the store robbed to get him out of his trouble. He figured it was no harm to Paden because the stock was insured, and Malling was to get part of the proceeds. The idea was he'd get held up when he opened in the morning, and they'd tie him up and the clerk would find him. Malling took his part in jewels because, being in the business, he could do better with 'em than if they'd been sold to a fence. The package you got at the hotel was his share."

"Didn't the taxi man or Enbrook have anything to do with it?"

"Not a thing. Enbrook is just a young guy that met Miss Paden at the beach and fell in love with her, and afterwards he hung round the store because he saw her there sometimes. He wouldn't tell that. The taxi business was just an accident, but it upset the plan. Malling was unconscious and couldn't let the holdups know. They went there expecting to find him and found Paden instead, and he fought 'em and they knocked him off."

"But how did you trace this to Malling?"

"Malling lied when he said he was at O'Connel's. He wasn't known there. But he had been somewhere, so I asked around night restaurants and found one where they did know him. He had been there a lot with a girl named Irene Walger. I found out where she lived and went out to question her. She wasn't home but there were some letters to her in her mail box—only we won't say nothing about them letters. One of 'em addressed to her had another one inside it, but all it said inside was John V. Huber and the name of a hotel. I didn't know what that meant but I called up the hotel to see if Huber was registered there. He wasn't, but they thought he was expected.

"So then I wondered what would happen when Huber got there, and I figured I'd find out. I didn't want to go there myself because they might spot me as a cop, so I had you do it, and it turned out that that was the way Malling was to get his share. Of course there ain't no John V. Huber. Malling was to go there and register by that name and his cut would be there waiting for him. He wouldn't want to meet those guys after the robbery because he might be seen doing it. It might be he didn't even meet 'em before it. I figure he got the idea of being robbed, but who was to do it and how it was to be done was fixed up by Irene Walger."

"You worked this out well," I told him, "and deserve a lot of credit."

"Yeah? You tell 'em. When I write out a report it always reads like I'm a dumb guy that only happened to get the one they sent me after, and now that I've got to dodge Uncle Sam about them letters it'll read like I'm cuckoo."

MRS. WALDER'S DIAMONDS

Originally published in *Collier's*, November 18, 1933.

"You two write this down," said the captain of detectives. "Mr. Justin Walder, five-five-six Park Avenue, reports a diamond pendant valued at $11,500 took off his wife yesterday, it might be in Land & Ellison's department store or it might be in the tea-room of the Norcort Hotel. Get busy."

They wrote it down. Al Lamon was the smart one, Jerry Murlin the "dumb" one of their partnership. It didn't worry Jerry to be considered dumb. When he got an idea everybody was astonished by it, but they forgot right away that he had had it, so he did not lose his reputation for being dumb. "At that," he said sometimes, "a cop don't have to know anything. It's the people he asks questions of that have got to know something."

"I don't know how we're going to tackle this," Jerry said when they had got outside the station-house.

"You never do know," Al told him. "We got to see the guy that made the squeal."

They went to Park Avenue. Mr. Justin Walder lived in a monumental-looking apartment building. There were a lot of liveried attendants about who were not sure Al and Jerry ought to be admitted; but they finally decided it would be permissible. Then another servant showed them into Mr. Walder's living-room. Mr. Walder was distinguished, obviously wealthy, gray-haired and about fifty-five years old.

"How was this about the pendant, Mr. Walder?" Al inquired.

"Mrs. Walder went shopping yesterday afternoon with a woman friend. The friend is Mrs. Allison Sidd of 7 East 64th Street. Mr. Sidd is a friend and business associate of mine. The two women had tea together in the tea-room of the Hotel Norcort. From there they took a cab to Land & Ellison's, where they spent some time shopping. From there they again took a cab and Mrs. Walder returned home. On arriving here she missed the pendant."

"I guess we got to see Mrs. Walder," Al decided. "Don't you think so, Jerry?"

"Sure, we better see her."

"I'm afraid you can't see her," Mr. Walder objected. "Mrs. Walder is quite prostrated by her loss and is ill in bed this morning."

"We got to see her anyway," Al informed him.

Mr. Walder went in and consulted his wife, then returned and took them in to see her. There was a great deal of lace and a great deal of silk on a very large bed. Mrs. Walder was blond and pretty, about twenty-three years old. She looked prostrated, right enough.

"How was all this, Mrs. Walder?" Al inquired of her.

"I can hardly talk about it. I feel too dreadfully! The pendant was a present from my husband. I was with a friend, Mrs. Sidd, and we had tea at the Norcort Hotel. Mr. Sidd is a friend of my husband."

She told it exactly as Mr. Walder had. When she had finished, Walder remained to comfort his wife, and the two went out into the hall. A servant was waiting for them. Al went into the living-room where they had talked with Mr. Walder, and when he came out the servant showed them to the elevator.

"What now?" asked Jerry.

"We got to see Mrs. Sidd."

The Sidds lived in a gray stone house with many iron grilles. There were some more liveried servants. One of them showed them into a room where there was a painting over the mantel, and Al jerked his thumb at it. It was unquestionably Mr. Sidd. He was about fifty-five years old and looked wealthy and distinguished. Then Mrs. Sidd came in. She was some years older than Mrs. Walder. She was pretty—even more sweet than pretty.

"We come here about Mrs. Walder's pendant," Al informed her. "You tell us how it was."

"Mrs. Walder and I had tea at the Hotel Norcort," said Mrs. Sidd. "Afterward we went to Land & Ellison's."

She told it just as Mr. and Mrs. Walder had. They thanked her and the man in livery showed them out.

"That's a nice lady, that Mrs. Sidd," said Jerry.

"Sure she's a nice lady. Well, would you think there was any use of us going to the Norcort or to Land & Ellison's?" Al observed. "I don't think those two ladies were at either of them two places yesterday."

They were near Central Park, so they sat down on a bench to talk it over.

"That Mrs. Walder," Al said, "is too scared to suit her story. She wouldn't be that scared over eleven grand in diamonds, even if her husband did give 'em to her. She's scared of something else and I guess it's of how she lost 'em. I wouldn't wonder if Mrs. Sidd wasn't even with her."

"They all got the same story," Jerry objected.

"Sure. Mrs. Walder told that to her husband when she had to tell him why she didn't have no pendant. Afterward she called up Mrs. Sidd and told her what she'd told him. Probably all Mrs. Sidd knows about it is just that. I don't think, though, there's any real harm in Mrs. Walder."

"I don't," said Jerry.

"She's young and she's married to this guy about fifty-five years old and sometimes it might get kind of tiresome to her. She don't look to me, though, like she was in the habit of stepping out. She loves him or she wouldn't be so worried. Would you figure she met some guy and he copped her diamonds and she don't dare to tell her husband about it? Or how would you figure it?"

"She might," Jerry agreed. "But we better check up at Land & Ellison's and the Norcort. It might be them two ladies are just telling the truth."

"It ain't likely."

* * * *

They checked up at the Norcort and at Land & Ellison's, but Al was right. The doorman at the Norcort knew both Mrs. Walder and Mrs. Sidd, and was sure neither of them had been there on the day previous. The doorman at Land & Ellison's knew them too and was equally positive.

"Now we got to find out where they did go," Al remarked.

That was likely to be some job, and Jerry said so.

"Sure it's some job," Al agreed. "That's what we get our pay for. We got no place to start to find that out from, so we got to *make* a place. Most anybody that tells a lie puts a little truth into it to make it sound more natural, so probably Mrs. Walder put a little truth in hers. She put a tea-room into it and a hotel. We'll try the tearooms."

"Al, there's a lot of tea-rooms."

"We got a lot of time. Besides, we don't have to go to all of 'em. We don't have to go to none where Mrs. Walder might have met her husband or some friend of his or hers."

"We can't find out if she went to them places if we don't have a picture of Mrs. Walder."

"We got one."

Al produced it. It was a small photograph but an excellent likeness.

"I don't see how you got that," said Jerry.

"I wouldn't expect you to see. What did you think I went back into that room for, after we talked with Mrs. Walder?"

They went to fourteen tea-rooms but nobody recognized Mrs. Walder's picture. They tried seventeen hotels—and seven restaurants. At the eighth restaurant the proprietor recognized the picture.

"Yes; the lady has been here several times," he told them.

"With who?"

"With a very handsome and liberal gentleman."

"About fifty-five years old?"

"About twenty-five, I'd say."

"See here," said Al. "You do a favor for us. You come down to police headquarters with us while we talk to them down there."

The restaurant man went with them to headquarters.

* * * *

"We got this kind of case," Al announced in the bureau of identification. "This is a lady living on Park Avenue. Well, she met a guy about who, I guess, she didn't tell her husband, and we figure the guy lifted some diamonds off her. About twenty-five years old. Who have you got that might be doing that?"

"Plenty," the officer in charge told them. To prove it he produced a mass of photographs, and they examined them carefully.

"This is the gentleman," the restaurant man declared with certainty.

"Well, well!" the officer remarked. "Pretty Face Mulgan, and you boys didn't know that?"

"We know it now," Al countered.

The last address given for Mr. Mulgan was a Times Square hotel, but it turned out that he had moved to Riverside Drive; so the two went out there. The apartment building was ornate.

"Mr. Mulgan is asleep," the hall man told them, "and mustn't be disturbed."

"Why, we wouldn't disturb him. We'll just go up anyway. Say it's a couple of police officers."

The elevator took them up and a Filipino opened the door to them.

"You go downstairs," Al advised the Filipino, "and talk with that hall guy."

They went in and closed the door behind them. Mr. Mulgan was, in fact, in bed. The place was luxurious. He turned to them, on a lace-edged pillow, a face like that of a mature and beautiful child.

"Well, boys, what is it?"

"Well, boys, is right," Al informed him. "Kick in with Mrs. Walder's ice."

"Oh, that!" Mr. Mulgan spoke with unruffled calm. "Why, she gave me that pendant! Who made the squawk?"

"Her husband."

"Go back and tell him he don't know what he's starting. If he wants it on the front page of every sheet in town that his wife was up here in my place two hours, come back and make the arrest."

"We don't believe that."

"All right. Arrest me then. I've got my witnesses — a switchboard operator and two hall-boys and a doorman and a couple of others that saw her come up here of her own free will; and if she happened to leave any jewels here they're not here now, so you'll do no good by searching."

They looked at each other.

"How about it, Al?" Jerry inquired.

"He might be right," Al replied uneasily. "It looks like we would start a lot of trouble if we grabbed this guy."

"You would," said Mulgan. "So go away and let me sleep."

They were nonplused.

"It makes me sore," Jerry declared angrily, "to see a mug like this making a liar out of a lady like that Mrs. Sidd."

"Well," Al suggested, "we might fix his face so that he won't mash no more married ladies."

"That's an idea," Jerry agreed happily.

Mr. Mulgan got swiftly out of bed. He was wearing orange-colored silk pajamas.

"If you two bums lay a hand on me," he cried anxiously, "I'll have the shields off both of you tomorrow morning."

They advanced purposefully.

"You let my face alone!" Mulgan cried in terror. "My face! I quit. No woman's stones are worth my face. But they aren't here. I left them with a friend of mine. I'll have to phone him."

"Go to it," Al replied.

* * * *

Mulgan went to the phone and gave a Drydock number. "Two flat-feet—" he started; but Al held up one finger at him. "One flat-foot," Mr. Mulgan amended, "will be down there in about twenty minutes to get the stuff I left with you. Give it to him."

"That's right," Al commended him. "Just one of us—because Jerry is going down and get them stones while I sit here to see you don't do no other telephoning. This trip will rate a cab, Jerry. . . . You better get back in bed," he told Mr. Mulgan kindly.

Jerry departed and was gone just forty minutes.

"O. K.?" Al inquired when he reappeared.

"O. K." He showed the diamonds glittering in his huge palm.

"It's tough we have to let this Mulgan go."

"We'll watch him," Al said, "and get him later on for something else."

They went down in the elevator.

"Where were they at?" asked Al.

"It was a junk shop. The dirtiest old guy I ever seen. He had 'em in a safe in back."

"Well, we got to turn this in at the station-house, but first we better check up we got the right one with the Walders."

"How do you figure this really was?" Jerry inquired. "That Mrs. Walder never gave 'em to him?"

"I got how it was while you were gone," Al answered. "This was some time ago, a rainy day, and Mrs. Walder and Mrs. Sidd was at a matinée, and after, they couldn't get a cab. So Pretty Face was cruising in a cab looking for women, and he offered to take 'em home. That way he found out who they were.

"Then one time afterward he met 'em, as they thought by accident, but it wasn't that; and so he got Mrs. Walder to meet him several times alone. There ain't no harm in her, in my opinion; she's silly and she thought it was adventure. So yesterday he got her to go to tea at some friends' of his, but where he took her was to his place. He had his witnesses ready. She got away, but not before he snatched the pendant off her. He thought she'd never dare to make a squawk."

"I thought he snatched 'em off her. The chain is broke. Well, anyway, we got the rocks," Jerry remarked.

"Yeh, but this business ain't going to be so pleasant. It's going to get both them women in wrong with their husbands."

When they got to Park Avenue, Al started to pay off the cab.

"Better keep the cab," Jerry advised.

They went up to the Walders'. Mr. Walder was at home. He was with Mrs. Walder, who, in negligee, was lying on a long chair. She looked at them apprehensively.

"Well, we got them stones," Al announced, "if this is the right one."

He showed it. It was the right one.

"Excellent work!" Mr. Walder commented. "Who had it?"

Mrs. Walder put her hands over her eyes.

"We found it in the cab," Jerry said.

Al's jaw dropped and Mrs. Walder raised herself upon her chair, her face filled with astonishment.

"What cab?" she asked.

"The cab you and Mrs. Sidd took in front of Land & Ellison's," said Jerry. "We got to turn it in at the station-house and you'll get it later."

Mrs. Walder sank back with color in her cheeks.

They went down in the elevator.

"That was a hot idea you had, Jerry," Al complimented him.

"Well," Jerry said, "I hated to see us make a liar out of Mrs. Sidd."

They went out to the cab and Al looked at the license card. It said, "Antonio Moriscino."

"Well, Tony," Al remarked, showing the pendant, "we found this in your cab."

"You didn't find nothing in my cab!" Tony cried.

"Sure we did. It got lost off one of them two ladies you picked up yesterday afternoon at Land & Ellison's."

"I didn't pick up no two ladies!"

"Listen, Tony, you don't understand. We're a couple of police officers. You're going to do us a favor."

"Oh, if it's a favor," said Tony, mollified, "that makes it different. Now I remember them two ladies. Where did I take 'em?"

"You brought 'em here. So you come over to the station-house with us while we turn in our report how we found this."

They all got into the cab.

"Well," Jerry said with satisfaction, "that all came out all right. What'll we do with the reward, Al, if this Walder should give us any?"

Al reflected.

"We might give it to the Police Fund. We won't miss it when we get what *Mrs*. Walder is likely to send us."

CITY WISE

Originally published in *Collier's*, July 31, 1937.

"This case," O'Malley said, "is that lady that got murdered in her train compartment. Mrs. Enler her name was. She had been visiting in Chicago for a couple of months and she was coming back to New York and her husband was waiting in the station for her. She didn't get off the train. Well, then they found she had been strangled. They tell me there ain't much mystery about this case because the guy in the next compartment killed her, but we can't find that guy."

"Why are they sure he killed her?" I inquired.

"He took her traveling bag. This lady owned a lot of jewelry and was careless with it and she carried it in her bag. The idea is the guy in the next compartment saw it. She got murdered in the tunnel. When the train went in the tunnel the porter went to her compartment and got her bag. When they got in the station he took all the bags off of the car platform and put 'em on the station platform. Then the passengers picked out their bags. This guy pointed out his bag and Mrs. Enler's bag to a redcap. Then he took the two bags off the redcap and walked away with them."

"You must have a good description of him," I decided. "Nobody observes people closer than a train conductor."

"Sure, we got a swell description. The train conductor and the Pullman conductor give us how he looked and how he was dressed and the porter described the bags. He looked like this."

He had a photograph.

"His picture?" I inquired.

"Not his. Eight other guys. The two conductors went to headquarters and looked at about a thousand photos to try and find a picture of him. Well, they didn't find none. So then they picked out a picture of a guy that had his kind of nose, and another one that had ears like his, and one that had his eyes, and others that had his other features. Then the photographer put all them features together and made this picture, A lot of cops been working on this case and the picture ain't helped 'em none. I guess I got to go and talk with all them train people."

* * * *

We saw the Pullman porter.

"You see the guy in the next compartment talking with that lady?" O'Malley asked.

"Yes, seh. She talk with plenty gentlemen. It seem like all the time some gentleman sitting talking with her with her compartment door open."

"You figure she knew them guys before she got on the train?"

"It don't look to me like she knew 'em. She look to me like a lady who don't like to be lonesome when she travel."

We found the husband at his home. He was wealthy and about fifty-five years old. There was a painting of his wife in the room where we interviewed him. She had been extremely pretty.

"Your wife in the habit of talking with strangers when she traveled?" O'Malley asked him.

"I never knew her to. She seems to have done it this time. It was a terrible mistake."

"How old was this dead lady?"

"She was twenty-six," Mr. Enler said.

"Maybe she knew that guy that had the next compartment."

"I don't believe she did. Gentlemen, you are making a mistake if you look for any motive for my wife's murder except robbery. Like other women who own a great deal of jewelry, Mrs. Enler forgot how valuable it was. I have no doubt that, in opening her traveling bag for some purpose, she carelessly displayed the jewels."

The police had found two of the passengers who had talked with Mrs. Enler. We saw them at their hotels. The first one was named Wilmant. He was a round-faced, red-haired youth with a look of perpetual astonishment. He had got into conversation with Mrs. Enler when they sat at the same table in the diner.

"You go and talk with her in her compartment?" O'Malley asked him.

"Yes—afterward."

"That lady act to you like she might be afraid of something?"

"I didn't notice anything like that."

The other passenger was named Cantwell. He was strikingly handsome and was in his thirties.

"I guess you went and sat in Mrs. Enler's compartment with her, too," O'Malley remarked to him.

"No; I didn't. I got into conversation with her in the club car just after leaving Chicago. I didn't talk with her afterward. I happened several times to pass through her car, and her compartment door was open, but there was always someone talking with her, so I didn't intrude."

"You think she knew any of those guys before or did she just meet 'em on the train?"

"I have no way of telling about that."

* * * *

"Well, O'Malley," I asked after we had left Cantwell, "what do you make of it?"

"I don't make nothing of it. What have we got? We got only a picture. I don't guess we'll ever find that guy. A cop can't find a guy unless he has some characteristic. If a guy's ears stick out, or he's got a flat nose, a cop can find him because he don't have to look only at guys whose ears stick out or have got flat noses. Well, the picture shows this guy has got no characteristic. He looks like a hundred thousand other guys. We got no other evidence. Nothing left in his compartment or in hers. No fingerprints in her compartment except the lady's and the porter's. No witnesses. That picture has been shown to all the attendants in the station, and to taxi drivers, and to clerks in hotels all around the station. They don't none of 'em recall noticing a guy like that. He ain't a guy that anyone would notice. A guy that looks like a hundred thousand other guys walks out of the station and loses himself among seven million people. We don't know who he is, or where he come from, or where he went. We got no way to find a guy like that."

"Do you think the picture looks like him?"

"It must look some like him. I guess if somebody knew the guy well, they'd know it wasn't his picture, but if somebody maybe seen him only a few times they might think it was."

"What are you going to do?"

"Do nothing—except I been thinking I might meet that same train tomorrow morning."

I thought it over but I couldn't see the sense in it.

"You're getting childish," I told him. "Why meet the train when the man got off of it two days ago?"

I met the train next morning. I wanted to see what this was all about. A lot of plain-clothes cops were scattered around the station and I finally found O'Malley.

"What's going on here?" I asked him.

The people were coming off the train and we stood and watched them. Then a redcap came, carrying a man's bag and a woman's bag. The bags were exactly like the ones the porter had described to us, and I started with astonishment when I saw the person following the redcap.

"Why, there's the very man you're looking for!" I ejaculated. "He looks exactly like the picture."

The man took the bags from the redcap in the station and went to the taxi entrance, and we followed him, but he didn't take a cab. He put the bags down and stood looking around, while a couple of cops talked with the taxi checker. Then he picked up the bags and went back into the waiting room and stood there, while the cops talked with the station attendants. Then he went to another station entrance but he still didn't take a cab. After a while he went to the main entrance of the station and stood on the sidewalk, while the cops talked with news dealers and to traffic officers and to the drivers of taxis which were waiting there beside the curb. Then finally he took a cab and we took another one and followed him with a couple of plain-clothes cops that jumped in with us, and a lot more cops crowded into another cab and came along behind us. We went to a hotel. A bellhop carried the man's bags in, and he had the boy put them down in the lobby and merely stood around, while the cops went around and questioned everybody. After a while one of the cops spoke to the man, and the man had another bellhop pick up his bags and they went to the other entrance of the hotel and he stood by the doorman.

"I begin to see through this," I told O'Malley.

"You're smart."

* * * *

We waited a long time, while the cops talked with everybody, and then the man took another cab and went to another hotel. It was tiresome because he repeated the same performance. He went in at one entrance of the hotel and waited, and went out the other entrance and waited, and the cops went around and talked to people. After a while he took another cab and went to a West Side ferry. We all went into the ferry-house and waited. Then we followed the man onto the ferry, and the cops talked with the ferry crew, and we got off again, and waited for the next ferry and got on it and got off again until we had tried all the ferries.

"No soap!" O'Malley stated.

O'Malley looked unhappy and the cops seemed discouraged and we went back to headquarters. I wasn't surprised that the man with his two bags went along with us, because I had guessed long before this that he was a cop.

"That didn't get you much, O'Malley," I remarked.

"Sure, it didn't get nothing."

"I understand what you've been doing. You couldn't find anyone who remembered the man when you showed them the picture, but you thought they might remember if they saw the man again; so you found a cop that looked a good deal like the picture and dressed him up the way the man was dressed and gave him two bags, and you had him stand around the station until you found someone who remembered seeing him before."

"Yeah, sure."

"Enough people remembered him so that you traced him through two hotels and down to the ferry, but at the ferry you lost him."

"I didn't think we'd find him."

I left O'Malley at headquarters but I met him the next morning. He had the woman's traveling bag that the cop had carried.

"What now?" I asked.

"I don't know nothing except to keep on going where that passenger went."

We went back to the railroad station and showed the bag to the attendants in the check rooms. It didn't mean anything to them. It didn't mean anything either, at the check room at the first hotel, but at the second hotel they brought out a bag almost exactly like it. It was Mrs. Enler's bag. We opened it but there was no jewelry in it.

"You're moving, O'Malley."

"We ain't getting nowhere."

* * * *

We went to the ferry but we didn't get aboard the boat; instead we went all around the neighborhood and rang doorbells and showed the man's photograph to whoever came to the door. We didn't have any luck. There was a little store that sold stationery and candy, and O'Malley went in to telephone headquarters that we hadn't found out anything, and I waited on the sidewalk till he came out. The street was full of kids and a kid about nine years old was sitting on the curb.

"You know that the lady in that store is giving away candy?" O'Malley asked.

"Sure," the kid said derisively.

"She is. You go in and you'll see."

The kid got up and went into the store. In about a minute he came out yelling, with a piece of candy in his mouth and another in his hand, and in about three minutes the store was full of kids and a hundred more were trying to get in. O'Malley stood at the door and when a kid came out he let another kid in, but first he showed the kid the photograph. The kids glanced at the photograph but they didn't know the man, but O'Malley let them in anyway. Then one kid knew him.

"Jim Murgin," the kid said.

"Yeah? Where does he live?"

The kid gave an address. We went to the address the kid had given us, and the landlady said Murgin had a room on the third floor. We had her go ahead of us and knock on the door and a hard-faced young man opened it.

"Okay, Jim," O'Malley told him. "Where's the dame's jewelry?"

"I don't know about no jewelry."

I could see that the man looked a little like the photograph. He was the right man and we finally found Mrs. Enler's jewelry in the stuffing of a chair.

"It is a remarkable piece of police work the way you have traced down this murderer. O'Malley," I exulted.

"I don't know if the guy's a murderer."

We took Murgin to the station house and he and O'Malley went into the captain's room. Then a plain-clothes cop and Enler came in, and afterward a cop brought in the Pullman porter, and some more cops came bringing the two passengers Wilmant and Cantwell, and they all went into the captain's room. Then they all came out of the captain's room and they booked Cantwell for murder.

"I don't see this, O'Malley," I declared. "If Cantwell killed Mrs. Enler why did Murgin have her jewelry?"

"You don't never see much. This case was this way: This Mrs. Enler liked sometimes to flirt. This Cantwell is one of them guys that hangs out with society people but has got nothing. Mrs. Enler was visiting in Chicago and she met Cantwell and flirted with him, and Cantwell took her seriously. Mrs. Enler seen Cantwell was serious about it and she got afraid of him. Cantwell had found out she was leaving and he took the same train without her knowing. After the train started, he found Mrs. Enler in the club car and begged her not to go back to Enler, but she wouldn't have nothing to do with him. Cantwell didn't have no chance to talk to her again until the train was in the tunnel coming into New York. Then he went to her compartment and she was alone there He had been getting more and more excited all through the trip and when she wouldn't talk to him he grabbed her and choked her. Well, he killed her."

"How did Murgin get into it?"

"He was in his compartment next to hers and he heard the fight going on in her compartment and he peeked out of his door and seen Cantwell come out. Then he went and looked in and he seen Mrs. Enler was dead. Well, Murgin wasn't giving no alarm about a murder and get himself maybe suspected by the police. He's a well-dressed, petty-larceny crook. He just went back in his own compartment and shut the door. Murgin had talked with Mrs. Enler in her compartment, and, like Enler said, she had opened her bag and he had seen she was carrying jewelry, but he says he didn't have no idea of stealing her jewelry till he was getting off the train. Then he seen her bag beside his on the station platform and it was so easy, he says, he had to do it. He went through a couple of hotels in case he might be followed and he took the jewelry out of the bag in the cab before he got to the second hotel and he checked the bag there to get rid of it. Then he went to the ferry to give the idea that he might have crossed the river and he walked home from there."

"I don't see how you figured all this out."

"I DIDN'T have to figure nothing out. All I had to do was find the guy that took the bag. It didn't prove he was the guy that killed her because he took her bag, but it looked like he knew that it was safe to take it. Here was a lady that got acquainted with so many people on the train that everybody noticed it. It might be she done that because she was afraid of somebody. The cops had got hold of two of the guys she talked with because Wilmant stopped to telephone after he got off the train and the dining-car conductor pointed him out to an officer, and the club-car steward give a description of Cantwell to the cops and he is the kind of guy that people remember and a taxi driver remembered taking him to a hotel. They both said they didn't know nothing about no murder. If this was murder for robbery, probably Murgin done it; if it was murder for something else, he maybe knew what. You can't call it only luck we traced him to the ferry by fixing up a guy to look like him, because even in a town as big as this one, the same people are likely to be in the same places at the same time of day. The news dealers and traffic cops and the hotel doormen and the bellhops all know what taxi drivers might be in them cab ranks at that time of the morning, and by pointing out the guy to everybody we was able to learn what cabs he took and where he went. I figured that picture we had made of him had to look a little like him even if it wasn't very much. Everybody we showed the picture to went and studied it. Maybe they thought at first they knew the guy, but after they studied it they decided they didn't and they wouldn't say nothing. I figured if somebody that knew the guy just looked quick at the picture, while maybe they was thinking about something else, they might think it was him and tell us. Well, how was I to get people to look at the picture without doing no thinking? While I was telephoning in that store it come to me. Them streets are full of kids and kids know generally who lives in their neighborhood. I give that old lady in the store a couple of dollars and told her to give every kid that come in two cents' worth of candy, and while they was all excited about the candy I showed 'em the picture, and one kid took a quick look at the picture and give us Murgin's name and where he lived."

"You're a psychologist." I told him.

"Not me! I was witness in a court case one time with some psychologists. They was nice guys but they didn't know nothing about people. . . . Well, we found the jewelry, which proved Murgin had took the bag, and to avoid a murder rap he told how it was he took it and that he seen Cantwell come out of Mrs. Enler's compartment, and when Cantwell found we had a witness against him he admitted that he killed her."

"An amazing piece of detection!" I decided.

"Yeah? I ain't never seen that word 'amazing' in a police report. You tell the inspector what you think of it, because now he's saying we was dumb or we'd have caught that killer quicker."

DECEIVING CLOTHES

Originally published in *Collier's*, September 9, 1942.

"We got a tough one," O'Malley said. "A murdered girl was found in a barrel in the East River. My idea, it's an Italian love-killing, but we might never prove it. In this kind of case nobody will tell a cop anything; then the cop gets a black mark. We got a name for this dead kid, but it might not be her right one, and cops pinched a suspect."

"Who's the suspect?" I asked.

"The guy's name is Gallo."

"How did they catch him?"

"Marks on the barrel showed it come from a wholesale produce house. Then a clerk at the produce house remembered a barrel like that had been carried away by an Italian. The guy peddles vegetables. The clerk remembered the name on the wagon said, 'L. Gallo,' and the license bureau give us the peddler's address."

We looked at the dead girl. She was plainly Italian and seemed in her twenties. She had been stabbed—small holes made by a stiletto. A label had been taken out of her coat and she wore a cheap ring with the letters "A" and "P" entwined in a monogram.

"What name have you got for this girl, O'Malley?" I asked.

"Antoinette Romano."

"How did you get it?"

"Cops showed this kid's picture to everybody around where Gallo lives and they all claimed they didn't know her. Then one cop got the idea he would show it to children, and one little girl said she'd seen that lady and pointed out where she lived. The landlady give 'em her name as Romano."

"What does Gallo say about it?"

"I ain't talked with him yet."

We went and saw Gallo. They had him locked up. He was a small man of about fifty, who scowled at us sourly.

"How would you feel," O'Malley demanded of him, "when cops made you look at that lady you murdered?"

"I feel okay, mister, because I never murder no lady. I am sell-a my vegetable. Two cops come in a car and say, 'Come along, you; you keel-a some lady.' I never keel-a no lady."

"Well," O'Malley remarked, "we won't get no information but I guess we got to go look at it."

We went to the East Side. The place was a tenement. Gallo had a small room in the rear of the basement which looked out on a court. In the court was a shed where he kept his horse and wagon. We saw the place in the hall where the police had found blood. They'd found none in his room. We examined the shed. There were boxes and crates there; there weren't any barrels. We talked with the tenants.

A young Italian couple named Carlucci had the basement rooms in front of Gallo's, and another young couple named Lero the room over theirs, and a youth named Vanutti had the room over Gallo's. There were other people above. The Leros and Vanutti came out on the stairs to see what was going on, while we questioned Carlucci. Vito Carlucci was plainly a fop; he was flashily dressed in a loud, striped suit. His wife was named Rosa. It was plain that she worshiped him. The Leros were named Tony and Maria. I never had seen a more beautiful girl than Maria Lero.

"Cops showed you that dead lady," O'Malley said to Carlucci. "You sure you didn't never see her before?"

"Sure I'm sure, officer."

"Well, you seen her too," he said to the Leros.

They shook their heads. "We never saw her before." Tony Lero informed us.

"She didn't ever come to see Gallo?"

"We don't know about that."

* * * *

We went all through the building and showed the girl's picture, but nobody knew her.

"A cop's got a fine chance!" O'Malley said bitterly. "They all know she got murdered and they'd say they didn't know her if she was their sister. We'll go see where she lived."

It was across the street and only a few doors from the tenement. A fat Italian landlady showed us the room. It looked out on the street. There were no woman's things in it.

"Cops took this kid's things," O'Malley remarked to me. "They didn't find much here—a little traveling bag and some underwear and a couple of dresses. Didn't that lady have any baggage but what the cops found here?" he inquired of the landlady.

"That's all, mister."

"How'd you know her name was Romano?"

"She said so."

"How long'd she lived here?"

"Two days."

"Well, O'Malley?" I asked.

"Well—nothing!" he told me. "She got killed in that building, but I don't know by who and I don't think we'll find out. I don't think it was Gallo."

"Why?"

"Why, you seen that dead kid and you talked with that Gallo. She didn't look to me like a girl that would be mixed up with that kind of guy. I don't think she lived in New York. I think she come here from somewhere else."

"Why?"

"The kind of coat she was wearing, if she lived in New York, would be bought at some big store. The coat wasn't new and the label wouldn't mean anything. Maybe whoever killed her took out the label; she might have did it herself. My idea, she didn't want people to know who she was. Well, if she come from somewhere else, where is her baggage?"

"What are you going to do?" I asked.

"Turn in a report I don't know nothing to do."

99

When we came out of the building, Vito Carlucci was standing across the street watching us. He turned and went quickly into the tenement.

"There's one thing you can do," I said. "You can watch Vito Carlucci. He's plainly a lady's man. His wife's much in love with him and no doubt she is jealous. I don't know what the situation may have been, but it's easy to imagine one in which a woman might embarrass Carlucci. There was blood in the hall but we found none in the rooms and it could have got in the hall as readily if she had been killed in Carlucci's room as if it had been Gallo's."

"You always got suspects."

* * * *

He went back to headquarters. I went there in the morning, but nothing was happening; so I went back there next day. I met him just leaving.

"Any progress?" I asked.

"I don't guess it is progress. We found a new landlady."

"How did you find her?"

"A guy told a cop on a corner that he had a room next to a girl that called herself Antoinette Romano. He seen the name in the newspaper."

I went along with him. The place was about half a mile from where Gallo lived. The landlady didn't want to let us in.

"Listen, lady!" O'Malley said to her. "You want I should send a couple of uniform cops around here three or four times a day to stand on your front steps asking you questions?"

She showed us the room. It faced on the street. There wasn't any baggage in it.

"Didn't that lady have a trunk or anything?" O'Malley asked the landlady.

"She had only a traveling bag. She took everything with her."

"How long did she stay here?"

"Three days."

There was a small restaurant across the street. We went across to it and O'Malley showed the girl's picture.

"This lady ever eat here?" he asked the proprietor.

"Not that I know of. The waiter will know."

He sent for the waiter, who looked at the picture and then shook his head.

"She never was in here."

We were leaving the place when I had an idea. "Do you know Vito Carlucci?" I asked the proprietor.

"Yes; he eats in here sometimes."

"There, O'Malley!" I exclaimed.

"You're good! We'll go talk with Carlucci, but I was going there anyway."

We went to the tenement. Carlucci wasn't at home but his wife Rosa was, and she seemed very nervous.

"Where's your husband?" O'Malley asked her.

"I don't know."

The young man Vanutti had come out on the stairs. "Carlucci didn't come home last night," he informed us.

"There's your case, O'Malley!" I cried. "Flight is one of the strongest proofs of guilt."

"Say! You get better and better."

100

We took Rosa to the precinct house for questioning. There was no one in the detectives' room, so we took her in there. O'Malley questioned her a long while, and she wept but she wouldn't say anything. Then a uniformed cop came in, bringing a suitcase.

"You find that guy you were looking for?" O'Malley asked him.

"Yeah, we found him all right, but we got there too late."

He put down the suitcase and went out again.

"Well," O'Malley invited me, "I and you'll go eat. You stay here," he told Rosa.

We went to a lunchroom. We were drinking our coffee when a police car with two plain-clothes cops in it pulled up outside. O'Malley went out and talked with them, and then motioned to me. We all got in the police car and drove to the tenement. We were getting out of the car when we noticed a taxicab that had just pulled away; so we jumped back in the car and followed it. It went pretty fast but we paid no attention to lights. When we'd almost caught up with it, a man jumped out of it while it was still moving and ran in between two buildings and we piled out and followed him. We searched a long while before we found Tony Lero hiding in one of the basements.

"Was it Lero who killed her, O'Malley?" I asked.

"Right—but I ain't got the whole of it yet."

We took Tony to the precinct house and O'Malley and one of the cops took him into the captain's office and I went into the detectives' room to wait for the end of it. Rosa Carlucci was still there and a couple of plain-clothes cops were with her, and Vito Carlucci was there too. They were just coming out of the room as I went into it. Then O'Malley came to me.

"I don't get this," I told him.

"That dead kid was Tony Lero's wife but his name isn't Lero. Panetta his right name is, and hers was Antoinette Panetta."

"A. P.," I declared; "on the ring."

"You said it! Tony and Antoinette and that pretty kid Maria that Tony was living with all come from Buffalo. Maria Biondo the kid's right name is, and she is married to a guy in Buffalo, about three times as old as her, who is called John Biondo. Maria and Tony got in love, and she left her husband and he left his wife, and they come to New York and called themselves Lero so nobody would find 'em."

"I see."

"Sure. Well, some Italian from Buffalo was in New York, and he seen Tony and Maria in that restaurant I and you went to. When he got home, he told Antoinette where he'd seen her husband. Well, the business stood this way: Antoinette hadn't got out of love with her husband because he'd run off with Maria; she wanted him back. First she made that Italian promise he wouldn't tell nobody else; then she sold all her things so she would have money; then she come to New York and got that room across from the restaurant where she could watch the restaurant."

"Why?"

"She figured if Tony and Maria had ate there one time, they might eat there again. After she'd been watching for a few days, she seen Tony and Maria go into the restaurant; so she waited till they come out, and she followed and found where they lived and she took that room we first went to, so she could watch the place. The afternoon she got killed, she seen Maria and Rosa Carlucci come out and go away somewhere; she'd been waiting for that. So then she went across to see Tony and carry out the plan she'd been figuring on."

"What was her plan?"

"Why, John Biondo, that Maria is married to, is one of them Italian boss guys that keeps everybody afraid of him. Quite a few times he's been suspected of murder, but they never could prove it. When Tony run away with his wife, Biondo give out to everybody that when he found out where Tony was, he was going to knock him off. So Antoinette give her husband his choice in the matter: Either he would leave Maria and go away somewhere with her, or she'd follow him and Maria wherever they went, and she'd send word to Biondo, and Biondo'd push Tony across."

"A clever woman!" I stated.

"What do you mean—'clever'? She got herself murdered. Tony's afraid of Biondo and in love with Maria; he couldn't see no way out of his trouble but to knock his wife off. Vito Carlucci heard 'em quarreling and come upstairs to see what the trouble was, and he opened Tony's door just in time to see the murder. So Tony told Carlucci, if he give out any information, he'd kill him. Tony's no soft guy, and Carlucci was afraid of him. Then Maria and Rosa Carlucci come back, and the dead girl was still there. So Tony told the Carluccis all about it."

"Didn't Gallo have anything to do with it?"

"His horse and wagon had to do with it; he didn't. That Gallo spends his evenings in wineshops; when he goes to sleep, he sleeps like a dead guy. They waited till everybody in the house had went to bed and Gallo was asleep. Then Tony and Vito took the girl to the shed and put her in a barrel they found there and used Gallo's horse and wagon to take her to the East River. They never thought of us tracing the barrel. Tony had took the label out of her coat because it showed she come from Buffalo, and the things in the room that had got blood on 'em they took along with 'em and left round in trash cans."

"Some case!" I ejaculated.

"Why, if we'd knew Antoinette was Tony's wife, there'd have been nothing to it. We couldn't find out about these people because they had no police records. Antoinette called herself Romano when she come to New York, so Biondo wouldn't learn where she'd went and follow her to Tony. Everybody around there believed Tony and Maria was married; they'd met all them people since they came to New York. We ain't yet found Antoinette's trunk; we'll find the trunk later. I figure, not knowing what she was going to do, she left the trunk with some express company; but just now, while we was questioning Tony, cops searched his place and found the stiletto."

"How did you learn all this, O'Malley?"

"Well, the girl got killed in that building. If Gallo didn't do it, then somebody else there did. You yourself seen Carlucci acted frightened and suspicious, and you thought that meant he done the murder. I thought it might only mean he knew who done it. We questioned him and his wife plenty, and they wouldn't talk; and in this kind of case, if people stand up like that under questioning, it's usually because they're afraid they'll get killed. I couldn't see no way to make Carlucci talk, but I thought we might make Rosa."

"That's a part of it." I declared, "which I don't understand."

"Yeah? Because you ain't the kind of guy that would look in some other guy's baggage."

* * * *

The suitcase was still there. I went over and opened it. Vito Carlucci's striped suit was in it, and there were cuts in the coat and it was covered with blood.

"What does this mean?" I asked, a little bewildered.

"Are you that dumb? First we picked Carlucci up and held him as a witness without anybody knowing it. Then we pretended to be looking for him. I and you brought Rosa in here and questioned her as to where her husband was. While we was doing that, a cop went to their place and got Carlucci's suitcase. We had give Carlucci another suit to wear 'so he wouldn't get his good clothes dirty,' and we cut holes in his coat and put some calf's blood on it. Then a cop brought in the suitcase. Then we left Rosa Carlucci alone with it. We knew she'd recognize the suitcase and be sure to look in it. While I and you was getting something to eat, cops took Rosa into the captain's office. She thought Tony had knocked her husband off to keep him from talking, and she handed 'em the whole story."

"The case could hardly have been solved in any other way," I decided. "O'Malley, you deserve commendation."

"Say! It's a pity you ain't the one that gives out those commends. The guys that do it would go blind if they tried to see me."